Mome

Kate prided herself on her self-control. She was as certain of that as she was of her distaste for the desires that she unfortunately stirred in men.

But Nicholas Monroe would not listen to her command to leave her house. He would not listen even when she told him that she was the bride-to-be of a lord whose brutal power Nicholas would do well to fear.

Instead, Nick took her in his arms, where Kate found herself on an overwhelming voyage of discovery. She met him kiss for kiss, yearning for yearning, following his every move with a passion she had never known existed.

Where had she been hiding, this wanton masquerading as a lady? How could she let this man take such advantage of her, when there would be so painful a price to pay?

But her questions would come later. Right now there was no question of what she wanted to do. . . .

Lady Kate's Secret

❧

by

Marcy Elias Rothman

A SIGNET BOOK

SIGNET
Published by the Penguin Group
Penguin Books USA Inc., 375 Hudson Street,
New York, New York 10014, U.S.A.
Penguin Books Ltd, 27 Wrights Lane,
London W8 5TZ, England
Penguin Books Australia Ltd, Ringwood,
Victoria, Australia
Penguin Books Canada Ltd, 10 Alcorn Avenue,
Toronto, Ontario, Canada M4V 3B2
Penguin Books (N.Z.) Ltd, 182–190 Wairau Road,
Auckland 10, New Zealand

Penguin Books Ltd, Registered Offices:
Harmondsworth, Middlesex, England

First published by Signet, an imprint of Dutton Signet,
a division of Penguin Books USA Inc.

First Printing, December, 1995
10 9 8 7 6 5 4 3 2 1

For
Ed Rothman
I care . . . a lot.

For
Ida Levine Elias
A fantastic role model,
before there was a name for it.

I am indebted and I owe more than I can say to Ilene Atkins, whose never-ending patience and good humor are a daily delight. Harold Brooks-Baker, of Burke's Peerage, London, has come to my rescue, and I can't thank him enough. Rita Lear and Irene Mayer can always be relied on to supply tea, scones, and sympathy. And thanks to Fay and Ed Ruby, who guide me and share my love of England

Chapter One

It was a night Nicholas Monroe would never forget.

The wind and rain pelted sideways forcing him closer to the mean buildings on either side of the fetid alley, his greatcoat and curly brimmed hat less than useless against the raging weather.

It was dark as death, and he cursed the demon that made him choose this night of all nights to venture so far from the lights and crowds of Drury Lane. No self-respecting duck would choose to be afoot, he groaned. For the tenth time since he'd arrived in London, Nick wondered what had possessed him to travel alone, without servant or companion. He had known full well that London wasn't going to fall at his feet in homage because he deigned to make it his new home, but he hadn't imagined the depth of isolation he would feel from the moment he landed on English soil.

Of course, I know why I came as I did, he thought. I wanted a clean start for Mam and me. I want to live like an English country gentleman and give Mam all she has missed. So what am I bleating about? A new beginning means a new life with new people. If I'm not making as much headway as I'm used to, it is no one's fault but my own. Who would ever expect Big Nick Monroe to be shy and awkward; but in London, however, the difference between home and England was roughly the equivalent of night and day, and of that no one warned him. Least of all his mother. How could he have known that a bloke couldn't just walk up to another man in a tavern, stand him a drink, and start exchanging lies as one would do in Sydney or

New York? In London this wasn't done, he found out to his chagrin the first night he arrived.

Nick could still feel his face redden at the picture he made buying a drink for a fellow next to him at a small tavern near his hotel. The man took the drink, but when Nick introduced himself and asked his name, the fellow left the drink and the tavern as if his britches were on fire. The landlord mopped the space in front of Nick and looked him up and down.

"Foreign, are you?" he asked, none too idly. "Best you know where you're drinkin', sir. And mind your back when you leave here. Now!"

Nick took the advice and departed soon after, his head spiraling in all directions, a cold patch between his shoulders, much like the way he felt in the alley tonight.

Nick wasn't at all sure, despite a great deal of thinking on the subject, what the landlord's warning was all about and, much as he wanted to, hadn't had the opportunity to ask. That was precisely the problem. There was no one so far to ask anything. The few times he'd requested more that street directions of servants at his less than palatial hotel, they'd looked at him askance, and he had soon given that up.

Hooper, his man of business, who handled his London banking needs, was called away a day before he arrived, and was not expected back for several more days. Nick would have to continue to fend for himself, however ineptly. He looked forward to Hooper's return as a mine of information on the way a gentleman got on in London. He never failed to ask himself what it was that marked him as a foreigner. He spoke the language as well, if not a great deal better than many other prosperous-looking men he'd overheard in the coffeehouses and theaters he had frequented in search of company, and yet they made him feel like a fifth wheel wherever he went. He never felt this way in the other cities and countries he'd visited, and that disturbed him.

What the hell is happening to me? Nick was not at all pleased with this loss of innocence, and in London, of all places. A man doesn't spent his life with a vision of heaven and then let a little unfriendliness make a mockery of dreams and ambitions, he thought, straightening his back and walking on purposefully. His spirits lifted with the sound of music coming from a ramshackle building on the right side of the alley.

Nick followed the sound of a small orchestra down a dark alley. He found the entrance and tried the door. It opened on a squeaking hinge, and he found himself in a dark, dank hallway with a dim light at the end.

He waited for someone to stop him, but no one appeared, and he ventured farther, coming into a lobby of a theater obviously fallen on hard times. The music had stopped, but ahead was a small stage with several people talking among themselves.

A group of musicians in the minuscule orchestra pit were being harrangued in German by a fat, angry man. Nick's attention was caught immediately by a tall young woman rehearsing by herself at the opposite end of the stage.

Nick lamented his limited knowledge of theater and music, but he trusted his instincts, and the speaking voice wafting above the harsh guttural sounds of the conductor was warm and lyrically enveloping. He moved forward quickly to hear more, but that was an excuse, and he knew it. He wanted to see the woman at closer range. The lush voice and romantic figure on the bare, dingy stage took his breath away.

A man on a hunt for a wife after years of denial studied every eligible candidate far more than others of his sex, Nick observed wryly, and this woman suddenly caught and held him as surely as if she had snared him with a spear.

What the hell is happening to me? he asked himself, falling heavily into the nearest seat on his third move forward, his eyes never leaving the stage on which his future bride continued to rehearse her lines to the total exclusion of all the ranting and theatrics that erupted around her.

With certainty, he knew that this houri with the red hair and Venus figure was going to marry him, and anyone who knew Big Nick Monroe would have agreed instantly.

The only problem he could see was that it was happening too soon, but that was a minor detail which would resolve itself in due course. In the meantime, he had no other thought except the actress. Every movement of the long legs under the plain but expensive gray woolen dress were, to his mind, liquid grace.

Nick shook his head in disbelief. He would have called himself the least poetic of men, and yet this woman on first sight was leading him to flights of fancy he didn't know were possible. Indeed, he wanted a wife, had come to England to find one among all the other things in his master plan, but to fall head over teakettle in love within the first ten days was far more than anything he could have bargained for. He wasn't sure he liked this loss of power over his good sense and the possibility that any woman—and an actress at that—might have him in thrall set him back on his heels. Nick Monroe didn't like this at all. He'd seen all he wanted to see of the hopelessness of love with his parents, and that was part of the reason he was in London and about to change his life forever.

He rose at once, determined to quit the place as quickly as he could. What was he thinking of, making a cake of himself over a piece of muslin he'd never seen before and hadn't even exchanged a word with? Fall in love with a voice and a figure, however glorious? Was he mad?

Nick was the first to admit that loneliness did strange things to people and no one knew better than he about loneliness. In his many journeys about the world in search of riches, loneliness was a constant companion. But it had never caused him to lose sight of an objective, and that was what he was doing now. London had plenty of respectable, eligible, and presentable females, and there was time to fix his interest with one of those. An actress! Of all things, they were to be avoided for anything but a bit of a romp.

At the back of the theater once again, Nick turned for a last look at the woman who had robbed him of his wits. He knew he'd been rocked profoundly by the hostility and coldness he had encountered in London, but was he so adrift in this most cosmopolitan city that the first woman he found wildly attractive could entrap him so easily?

Love at first sight? Ridiculous! Such a thing couldn't happen to a hard-headed businessman. Could it?

The Lady in Gray, as he called her, had come down to the footlights, her vivid eyes sparkling.

Nick flung himself into the nearest seat.

"Herr Hendricks, enough of your hysterics. We are here to perform." This time the creamy voice that had thrilled him from the first showed a commanding timbre, and the cast and musicians looked at her gratefully. Immediately they took their places.

Even to his untutored mind it was an extraordinary production, neither opera nor drama, but elements of both.

Nick was lost to the music and the drama and was only peripherally aware that someone had taken a seat behind him in the stalls.

"Sorry, Gov', but the tall lady takes exception to your presence. Follow me like a good chap, and nothing more'll be said." A rough voice, smelling of whiskey, spoke in his ear.

Nick was inordinately pleased to have caught the lady's attention, no matter how disappointing the result. He unfolded his long legs and took his damp coat from the seat next to him before following her messenger, however reluctantly.

At the stage door he pressed a coin in the tough's ham-sized hand, hoping to sweeten his tongue.

"When's the play opening?"

"No idea. Me job is keeping johnnies like yourself far away from the lady," he said, returning the coin.

"And the lady's name?"

"Haven't the foggiest, sir."

Nick handed him more money, hoping to jog the man's faulty memory. An entrepreneur himself, Nicholas Monroe knew enterprise when he saw it.

"Won't help. We calls her 'The Mystery Lady.' She comes and goes when she pleases, talking only to the management, doin' her role and leavin' right after a performance."

"Was this a performance then?"

"Right in one, sir."

Nick felt ridiculous asking the obvious. "But where was the audience?"

"Never is," the burly guard replied, urging Nick toward the door, expecting his answer to clear up the matter completely.

Nick was vastly amused and under other circumstances would have taken serious objection to being rousted by anyone as villainous as this fellow.

"Isn't that a bit odd?"

"She don't pay me to have opinions, so I'll say good night."

"Be a good chap and give me the lady's name," Nick coaxed, taking a cheroot from his case and offering it to the man.

"Look, you're not the first cove as wandered in here, and I'll say to you as I says to them, piss off. I hain't fer sale, and she hain't either."

Nick liked the rough chivalry. It seemed to say a lot about the actress. He would far rather have his feelings about the Lady in Gray confirmed by the tough man than by all the clerics of Christendom. Nick had learned early in his own harsh life to trust the judgment of such men on morals and character. It had, after all, helped him make his fortune. Nick tipped his hat at the fellow and went out to face the rain and wind with a lighter heart than he might have expected.

He had seen his future, and she was a woman he could worship.

Nick hadn't a clue about the fair lady's name or direction, knew less than nothing about the odd little theater where she seemed to reign for an audience of none, but something told him that time and luck would take care of all that. However, he reminded himself the last thing he needed at the moment was feminine distractions.

The piercing weather told him it was time for reality to

come back into his life, take matters into his own hands, and get his affairs in order.

He had lost precious time hanging about London like a lost sheep. Tomorrow he would correct all that.

Chilled and impatient to be away, displeased with herself and her performance, Kate Grovenor stood framed in the stage door; waiting for Barkley to assure her that the huge interloper had left the theater and the neighborhood.

Afraid of detection, her antennae were always up for any untoward movement in the house. An audience of one was as bad as a houseful, and set her nerves on edge. She hated all the histrionics that seemed as necessary as breathing backstage, and was only driven to it when she felt herself observed from across the footlights by anyone but others in the company.

Kate could not be sure how long the man had been in the stalls watching her before she sensed his presence. When she did, she wasted no time giving a prearranged hand signal to good and faithful Barkley. It was all that had ever been needed to have the one or two intruders removed with a minimum of disturbance. Thank heaven there had been few of those. Even so, Kate had managed to get a fleeting look at broad shoulders and luxuriant dark hair and the clear outline of a man even larger than Barkley.

Now shaking with cold and strain, she resolved for the hundredth time to give up her dream life. It was more trouble than it was worth.

Kate smiled, knowing it was a useless exercise to pretend that she could ever give up acting voluntarily. Something so important to her soul, which more than incidentally gave poor and talented people a forum for their varied talents, was all that stood between her and a life that was increasingly unrewarding.

Why her life was becoming burdensome was in some ways as mysterious to her as it would be to any onlooker, Kate was forced to admit. With London at her feet, or so her friends were quick to tell her, what, in heaven's name, could any sane twenty-six-year-old woman want? No one had to tell her most women would give their eyeteeth to be in her shoes. If that's supposed to chasten me, it does, but it doesn't make me ecstatic either, Kate acknowledged ruefully.

Kate longed to tell someone about her theatrical ambitions, but they would have laughed her up one side of London and down the other, and she couldn't bear that. Was she rapidly becoming a malcontent with aspirations so far out of reach as to be absurd even to her own mind? Kate cringed. She hated self-pity, and what else was she indulging in, if not that? Was she becoming insufferable?

Kate knew silence about her double life was the only protection she had against public ridicule. Honesty was something she could not afford. She would have to be content with dreaming of Herr Hendricks's latest inspiration, which meant a new and challenging role was once again rattling around in the gnome's head.

Now in livery, Barkley drove her black carriage into the alley. Tall as she was and swathed in a capacious cape, Kate managed to bound into the carriage and order her coachman to spring the horses. She had dawdled enough, and didn't dare be missed.

Nick Monroe stepped out of a doorway, his face pale and drawn, cursing under his breath. The pristine coat of arms shining on the door of the smart carriage spelled the end of his naïveté.

By the look of it, she was a grand society lady, or a courtesan that someone far more exalted than he had captured before he ever set foot in London.

He was out of luck, and no mistake.

Chapter Two

The estate manager waited in the forecourt of Delacourt House, fingers crossed, his attention glued to the studded front door.

Matt Meredith's dreams of a peaceful old age rested on the handsome young man he'd just led through fifteen bedchambers, six reception room, and all the nooks and crannies of the venerable old mansion which had been his life from boyhood. The dear lad inside the house might be a foreigner, even odd in his ways, but he spoke the King's English like the gentry, and that was good enough for him. Matt liked the man on sight, and would have laid a monkey, had he had that much money, that the newcomer knew what he wanted, and no mistake.

Matt's fervent hope was that Mr. Nicholas Monroe wanted the estate despite its decay and dilapidation. Neglected for years by a family whose extravagance and negligence had caused their own downfall, and who didn't give a damn for their tenants' welfare, Matt, as the family's agent, was forced to extort rents from good and honest estate workers for employers he and they had grown to hate.

Rent collection was the blackest time of his life, and when he received a letter from old Winters, the family solicitor, saying that he was coming down from London with an interested party, Matt couldn't believe it. The gnarled, white-haired manager prayed that the crafty solicitor wasn't going to ask a mint for the estate or otherwise try to gull the young Australian, for something told him that Mr. Winters would catch cold at it.

His hands trembling from anxiety, Matt took an ancient

crusted pipe from his corduroy hacking jacket, finding
scant consolation in the way the light of a glorious spring
evening bathed the red brick, Jacobean house he loved only
a step behind his wife.

At last his vigil was rewarded. The massive front door
opened and Monroe emerged smiling, the lawyer folding
papers into a leather folio, snorting and swearing, obviously
not at all pleased with the business at hand. Matt hurried toward them.

"You have stolen a great property," Winters said sourly,
impatient to be off and rid of a burden. "The family will not
thank me for this day's work, I can assure you."

"You may have learned a powerful lesson this day,"
Nick Monroe said, his voice grim. "England's colonies may
be dumping grounds for the people the crown thinks unfit,
but many of those misfits will one day turn around and bite
you English on the arse, as I did today."

"I beg your pardon—" the old man spluttered.

"You may indeed." Nick was enjoying himself. "I know
more about the potentialities of this property than you do.
I didn't come here with down on my cheeks, much as you
would like it to have been the case. I was prepared to pay a
great deal more. I wanted this place for reasons of my
own."

The lawyer turned apoplectic with outrage.

"You young fool. This is nothing but a white elephant,
and good riddance to both of you."

The bent figure stumbled toward the stables. Nick with
an enigmatic smile on his face, was suffused with a glow of
triumph. Winters never suspected. It was clear the old scandal had slipped his mind. Good. The name Monroe seemed
to mean nothing to the old bounder, and that suited Nick.

Buying the house he'd heard about all his life, putting
one over on Winters, one of his father's persecutors, was
the second most satisfying encounter in England. It was all
he needed to feel wholly himself once again. Or almost so.
No amount of preoccupation with details and grandiose
schemes could erase the magnetic pull of the Lady in Gray,
who had captured his imagination as no other woman. He

was annoyed that he'd been unable to get the picture of her or the thought of her out of his mind since the night in the derelict theater.

Matt Meredith watched the play of warring emotions on Nick's face and wondered what manner of man this was who could humble the mighty Winters, the misanthrope who had made his own life a torture in the name of serving the despicable Delacourt family. Would he have to endure more of the same from this man, or could he trust his first impression of Nick Monroe as a fair but firm man with a fellow feeling about Delacourt House? He got his answer soon enough.

"I am putting you in charge of restoring the house and grounds as they ought to be, and don't worry about the cost," Nick Monroe said, shaking off the sudden gloom that had overtaken him.

Matt grinned like a boy.

"Don't get too happy too soon, Matt," Nick cautioned. "I will be back here in a few weeks with my mother, so you have to move very quickly and make this place habitable. Can you do it?"

"You did say money was not to be thought of?" Matt held his breath.

"Within reason," Nick cut in quickly. "I never dictate terms to a man I give authority to act in my name. I trust that he knows the ground better than I do and will use his best judgment in my behalf. But don't make the mistake of thinking me a fool with my money. I didn't come by my fortune through stupidity or indolence."

Meredith felt sure he'd died and gone to heaven. A reasonable and generous man was more than he'd dared hope would be his lot for the rest of his natural life.

"Winters gave me the original designs for the house, and I wish you to follow them to the letter. I will select a London artisan who will work with you. Just keep me informed of your progress. Not your difficulties, your progress. However, I am a day away, and I can help you when difficulties become impossibilities."

The manager nodded in agreement, and the two began to

walk toward the stables, the beginnings of a perfect understanding taking root.

"Your authority, Meredith, extends to firing the present butler and housekeeper and hiring a new staff. It is a lesson I wish you to convey to others. I will not be treated as a foreign parvenu. I was born in London and have seen much. I am not easily fooled."

Matt understood at once. It gave him immense pleasure to accede to everything Nick Monroe wanted, for the butler and the housekeeper, diligent spies for Winters, had added measurably to his miserable existence for more years than he cared to remember.

A stable hand had anticipated Nick's departure and had his hired curricle waiting, all sleek and far more presentable than when Nick arrived.

None of this was lost on him. Extraordinary service such as the stable lad had shown came from above, and he knew with certainty that he had backed the best man to bring the estate back to its onetime glory.

"I look forward to a long and happy life at Delacourt House," Nick said gaily. "I trust you to help me."

Indeed, Matt Meredith thought he'd died and gone to heaven.

Chapter Three

It was five o'clock on a gray and grainy dawn, and the annual ball at Holland House, a crush of more than usual proportions, or so it seemed to Lady Katherine Grovenor, was mercifully coming to a close.

Her cousin, Lizbeth Grovenor, an old dear who was jokingly called her chaperon, had slept through most of the ball, as usual. At three o'clock she pleaded a sick headache, and Kate sent her back to Grovenor House, assuring her that her father would escort her home.

Her father's ancient cousin was an undemanding duenna. All the poor spinster wanted of life was peace, quiet, and a luxurious roof over her sparse, gray head. All this suited Kate down to the ground. She could observe the proprieties, and yet have the freedom she needed for her special life. A curious or more conscientious companion would not have suited Kate at all. As for her maid, a young Irish lass, Kate had no fears. Dina Casey was the soul of loyalty and sympathy.

Now surrounded by a phalanx of beaux waiting for the signal honor of escorting her home, Kate looked around in vain for her father. She had no intention of going home with any of her suitors without Lizbeth in tow. The need to keep smiling, the de rigeur pleasantries and smart retorts and pithy comments, almost all deadly and critical, no longer challenged her, indeed, had long since begun to set her teeth on edge.

In God's name, whatever made me think all these trappings of sophistication mattered two pins? She couldn't deny that she had welcomed, delighted in the cultivation of style and manner, dress, air, and the correct tone of ennui expected of a lady of fashion. In truth, Kate admitted, she loved every moment until a year ago, when she realized the utter futility of wasting her life on finding a husband and other trifling pursuits. Her disillusionment rose with the length of the list of shams that had been the center of her life for so long.

Her escorts, fighting to get closer to her, startled Kate and brought her back to the moment.

"Do form a search party for my sainted father." She laughed, knowing full well that they would move in a body to comply with her wish.

It didn't do much for Kate's humor to know that her father had forgotten all about her five minutes after she had begged him to take her home hours ago.

What with talk of politics, horses, gambling, and especially women, the four corners of his life, Pearson Grovenor, the Earl of Keene, had little time for his daughter and only child. He had told her often enough that the only use she served was allowing him to bask in the role of fortunate parent of the most sought after woman of the *ton*. The subject came up only when it reflected on a crony whose daughter was not as successful as Kate.

She didn't often think about her father's less than generous qualities as a parent. She had made a life of her own and had learned not to think of his neglect. In truth, Kate often went to great lengths to collaborate in it. Her father's disregard, after all, had enabled her to pursue her stage life with little intrusion.

But one touch of scandal would change all that. Her father was an implacable foe when he judged his dignity or his family name compromised. The very idea sent a cold chill down her back. Her imagination could picture what would happen if Pearson Grovenor and society learned she lived a second life as an actress and singer. Almost worse was her support of Herr Hendricks and the company with which she had performed for the past year with the assistance of Barkley's indispensable guile.

Kate was well aware that her recent fear of detection was

becoming close to mania, but she was afraid that her father would marry her off or relegate her to the countryside if he knew about her second existence.

It was the sight of the dark-haired giant that Barkley had ejected. The possibility that he had been in the theater and might recognize her or tell anyone she knew sent Kate into a tailspin.

For a long time Kate had not worried about this, the most important aspect of her life, content to enjoy the deception in gossip-crazy London. If her frequent absences made her old cousin and father and romantic-minded friends assume she had an innocent rendezvous with any of the hopeful men who filled her dance cards and kept the Grovenor House full of fragrant reminders of their affection, that suited Kate's deception. The very idea fit perfectly with the carefully crafted public persona she had contrived over the years: a siren of epic proportions. Only Kate knew she was the last woman to deserve the title. Far from it. She was scared green at the thought of physical affection or intimacy. Indeed, she froze at the slightest touch, especially from people she disliked.

Kate was again so lost in her own thoughts that a hand placed heavily on her bare shoulder made her cringe, and she discarded it with force.

"What is this?" a slim, saturnine-looking man asked, his voice pitched low and suggestive in Kate's ear. "Surely I, of all people, cannot be repugnant to you."

You deserve boiling in oil, she wanted to say, but didn't. She had to keep her tongue between her teeth where Lord John Peterbroome was concerned. The leader of London's most disreputable set, he was a rake and a mean gossip, and sensible people learned to keep him at a distance if they could. He had been ruined by his family from birth and by an endless line of women who loved getting too close to the flame. They longed to be the next chatelaine of a huge Scottish castle when Peterbroome's tyrannical grandfather died and he inherited. But each lady and hopeful family had learned to regret setting their sights in his direction. He was none too pretty in his manners and morals, and many hearts were badly bruised and disillusioned.

"You're not attending me, Katherine," he said angrily, forcing her face toward him with a long, prehensile finger.

Kate made no secret of her displeasure. It was clearly an act of possessiveness that no other man in London would dare. Admirers who had replaced those sent to find her father didn't hide their consternation at the liberty. All knew Kate was fastidious and disliked to be handled. Many who crossed the line into public intimacy suffered a look or setdown from a mistress of the art.

Kate was seething. What is it about me that every last lecher in London wants to make me the object of his attentions? Could the rumor be true that the betting books at the clubs held wagers on who would finally capture Kate the Elusive? The idea appalled her. Perhaps her father and her friends were right after all, and it was time she thought about marriage. Perhaps I overstayed my time on the London scene. Perhaps I have become fair game for men like Peterbroome just to win a bet and the questionable esteem of their friends.

Peterbroome pushed everyone aside and took Kate roughly by the arm. "I told your father he has spoiled you rotten, given you too much freedom, and you need a firm hand. I propose to be the one to do it."

"How dare you speak to me so familiarly?" Kate reared back in horror. "Spoiled? Because I won't succumb to your charms or bullying arrogance the way others do?"

Kate glared, indignant, her skin crawling at his touch.

"Take your fangs and be gone," she said loudly, removing his hand, knowing those around them would hear and spread the word over London by lunchtime. If he thought to claim her, he had thrown down a challenge Kate would be only too happy to accept.

The gasps that had greeted her sally reminded her where she was, and she regretted that she had allowed Peterbroome to goad her into folly. He was a bad enemy, and she knew it, but wild horses couldn't make her take it back.

Peterbroome stalked off with as much dignity as he

could manage, running blindly into two women who were heading toward Kate. He pushed past. The lovely blond woman resting on a cane was Lady Barbara Maitland, the much-loved and admired wife of Captain Tarn Maitland, one of the most influential men in Whitehall and the City. The other was the outspoken, statuesque Lady Colby Browning, the wife of an important man in the Foreign Office, Lord Nevil Browning. Where Colby was tart-tongued, irrepressible, Barbara was quietly brilliant and gentleness itself. They were like older sisters to Kate, and she adored them. For a number of years they had befriended her and given her wise counsel, even if she didn't always take it. As much as she admired them, she was unable to confide the existence of her clandestine life.

The older women heard and came quickly to Kate, trying to head off more fodder for the wagging tongues of the *ton*.

"My dear, do allow us to see you home." Lady Barbara was the first to speak, taking Kate's hand and pulling her forward. "Tarn and Nevil deserted us hours ago."

Colby Browning imperiously cleared a path for the three of them. Kate was grateful for their intervention and followed meekly. Barbara and Colby were her idols, and she laid much of her growing discontent with the emptiness of her life to the standards they set. They were mainstays of society, models of contented domesticity. Kate longed to learn the secret of their happiness.

Kate hesitated to breathe a word about her theatrical aspirations to these exemplary wives and mothers, fearing their disappointment. Actresses and singers were to be admired at a performance, but socially they ranked not at all. She could not bear disillusioning Barbara and Colby. Pillars of society steeped in good works without self-righteousness, Kate was happy to assist them in every way. Like everyone else, Kate knew they married for love, and urged her to do the same. They warned her that someone like Peterbroome, seeking to make a name for himself in the clubs, would one day come along and ruin her reputation. Butterflies have short lives, they warned her.

"Barbara and I insist on talking to you again about getting married," Colby said in her forthright way when the Browning carriage set off from Holland House.

"Surely, my dear Kate, you must have met among that army of suitors of yours someone who can make you happy?" Barbara Maitland asked.

Kate shook her head and decided to be honest with her friends, or as honest as she dared. "No man has yet made me want to make him the center of my life the way Tarn and Nevil seem to be yours," Kate said. Was she the only one out of step? Need a man be the only answer to her future? What's wrong with me? Kate wanted to ask her friends, but was afraid of making a fool of herself.

The women looked at each other. They sensed Kate's unease, but not its cause. An uncomfortable silence reigned for the rest of the journey.

Kate welcomed the respite, allowing her mind to single out all the reasons the thought of marriage was so painful, indeed not to be thought of for a moment.

When Kate had seen of her parents' marriage gave her a distaste for the institution that amounted to fear.

Kate's father's many failings, especially his infidelities flaunted like a flag unfurled in front of her mother, had given Kate a wretched childhood. No child of hers would ever be subjected to the role of message bearer between two volatile people who could hate each other one moment and often tumble into bed a quarter-of-an-hour later as if nothing more untoward happened than a disagreement about the brewing of a cup of tea.

Long after her mother died, Kate could still remember the holy wars between her parents, amounting to a litany of inconsequential and monumental matters that Pearson and Deidre Grovenor could find to argue about. Oh, no, Kate promised for the hundredth time, shrugging off her earlier doldrums, no man will ever have the power to make my life a living hell the way my father had made my mother's.

In truth, Deidre Grovenor had been no angel. Kate knew better than anyone that her mother was often the most impossible, faithless creature ever created, albeit beautiful and enchanting, and a wonderful companion when the spirit moved her, which wasn't as often as her only child would have liked.

The sound of the carriage pulling up before the white five-story Grovenor town house brought Kate out of her reverie with a jolt. She kissed Barbara and Colby.

"Pray for me. I am not sure of anything anymore."

Chapter Four

Nick Monroe cursed himself for taking so long over dinner in the dreary posting house on his way back to London.

On the other hand, he thought, after finally regaining his seat in the curricle, the time taken over an inedible mutton dinner laced heavily with the good brandy he carried in his flask for such purposes had been well spent. He felt only slightly less murderous.

Nick had arrived in a tearing rage after the interview with Winters. Instead of placating the old crook to insure immediate possession of the estate, he should have strangled him with his bare hands. The memory of the afternoon holding back his enmity for the gnarled villain reanimated, making Nick's long, slim fingers tighten into fists and his nerves scream for release.

When the money for Delacourt House was exchanged, he would settle old scores. The people who had ruined his parents' lives and damaged his youth would pay dearly, Nick promised, and none more so than the solicitor.

Nick gave the horses their heads, and they departed the shabby stables in unseemly haste, leaving clouds of dust in their wake. The road stretched ahead in the early evening light. Nick had every intention of returning to London without another pause. Although, what the hell am I returning to? he growled.

Try as he could, the feverish activity of the last few days had not in the least slaked his desire to see the Lady in Gray again and settle once and for all time who and what she was. The mystery surrounding the woman haunted his days and nights. If she or the henchman thought they'd seen the last of Big Nick Monroe, they were sadly out. Like the completion of the sale of Delacourt House, she was unfinished business, but not likely to remain so. He'd find her, no matter how long it took.

Shutting out all else, Nick recaptured in every particular the way the actress looked, lithe and commanding, the Nile-green eyes drenched in melancholy when she rehearsed her lines in the seductive voice at the side of the stage and then blazing like two fireballs, demanding the play resume. Etched forever in his brain were the perfectly rounded breasts against the fine wool cloth, every indentation and delicious curve of her body, the titian hair, all could be summoned at will, as he was doing now. Nick's desire for the actress grew each hour, each day, and he groaned into the approaching night, abandoning himself, begging for the sight and feel of the only woman who had ever brought him to his knees.

Darkness lit by a full moon descended moments before he heard the anguished cries of the horses. Rocketing back to the moment, he needed to use all his strength to keep the grays from bolting.

"Stand fast and deliver."

Nick heard the muffled voice of a masked rider atop a nervous stallion shouting above the unholy din.

Every nerve, every instinct rose to blind Nick with fury. Damn England anyway! Nothing had gone right since he'd come home, and this, caught napping like the greenest country bumpkin, was the last straw. The boomerang Nick had lodged in the curricle cushion, more as a souvenir than defense, was only a hand span away. Not many Australians had possession of one, but Nick did. He'd never thought to have need of it, but he'd be damned if he would lie down abjectly for some cowardly highwayman without giving a good Australian account of himself.

"Steady on, mate," Nick called out, leaning over as if to make himself heard. The last syllable was barely out, the boomerang launched, when the holdup man disappeared from view.

The next minutes were all confusion. Nick caught the boomerang on its return, leaping from the curricle at almost the same moment and brandishing a gun in the other hand, only to find the thief sprawled at his feet, his horse wheeling off in the darkness.

"A bloody boomerang." The highwayman was laughing so hard he was doubled over, his mask hanging over one ear, his hat falling over his face. He hiccupped. "Only I could make such a mull my first time as a brigand."

The man's laughter was so contagious that Nick could do no more than join his attacker on the ground, laughing uncontrollably as well. They were so overcome with the absurdity of it all that neither could do anything more than roll around in the dirt clapping each other on the back like long lost friends.

"You bloody Britishers are past understanding," Nick said at last, taking a flask from his pocket and passing it to his now unmasked friend.

"Carrying a bloody boomerang, old son, is not very sporting," the Englishman drawled, lifting the flask, seemingly content to remain drunkenly spread-eagled on the ground. "You must be one of those Australian chappies."

All at once Nick's laughter died in his throat. The bumbling highwayman spoke with the most negligent of public school accents, the kind of voice and man who had made Nick's long-awaited fantasy of living in London a bleeding nightmare. Men like this bastard treated him like dirt under their feet at the opera and theater, looked through him as if he didn't exist when he walked along Bond Street, looked askance when he stood transfixed before their clubs, their houses, and their beautiful women.

Until that moment, Nick hadn't been aware of anything about the man, didn't care to, yet the situation was so ridiculous that the chance to have the first real, hearty laugh in weeks had erased all else from his mind. There was enough light from the moon for a good look at his erstwhile assailant. It changed matters at once. The man could not have been more than five and twenty, a few years younger than he. Dressed in the height of fashion, with a fine fawn coat over well-muscled shoulders, an athlete's legs in skin-tight brown breeches, a slim face that spoke of centuries of breeding and forelock-pulling tenants, confirmed Nick's suspicions. He'd been held up, however unsuccessfully, by a goddamned fop with a prejudice against Australians.

"You, who would have shot me between the eyes if you could have sat your horse, talk about the sporting thing?" Nick roared ferociously. Getting to his feet, he took back his flask. "What the hell did Australia ever do to you except take your criminal flotsam and jetsam or poor sods who didn't have the price of an honest solicitor?"

Nick stormed toward the horses. Long practice and burning ambition had taught him to use his temper judiciously. Nick hadn't been so agitated in years, frustrated at every turn by everything and everyone he'd encountered since he landed. Nick was afraid he'd explode. His fists itched to settle old scores, and the inept, sodden excuse for a Regency Beau at his feet was as good as anyone to vent his spleen on.

Nick turned and saw the man trying to rise to his feet. He was hurt, and his legs wouldn't hold him. He fell and rose again, unaware that Nick was watching him.

"Take my hand," Nick offered.

"I'd rather not," the posh voice said, the exertion beginning to take its toll, his face damp with perspiration, the earlier laughter dead on the freshening breeze that was blowing in from the north.

"I'm your prisoner. The local justice of the peace is a few miles back on your left. He's a friend of the family, but that won't cloud him to his duty."

Nick insisted on helping the man to his feet.

"You are more of a clunch that you look," Nick said, his anger evaporating. "You didn't harm me."

Nick helped him into the curricle, running his hand expertly over the fellow's ankle for signs of broken bones. In the world Nick came from doctors were few and far between, and Nick had learned skills and arts that endeared him to his men and saved his many enterprises costly delays.

"I never meant to hurt you. Far from it. Actually, I rather hoped you'd kill me."

"That's a bit of a facer," Nick jeered. He hated extravagant emotion in men. He came around the curricle and took up the reins.

"My name's Charlie Slayton," his passenger offered, staring ahead. "I'm bankrupt, and my folly tonight was to get enough money to emigrate, or get killed in the attempt. It didn't much matter which, and still doesn't. I don't expect you'll believe me."

"Get your courage out of a bottle?"

"Many bottles, actually."

Nick turned to study this strange man. Farfetched as the story sounded, he believed every word of it. He'd met too many Charlie Slaytons, high-born, misfit remittance men sent out to the colony to escape scandal or the gallows, often both, but really to insure the preservation and sanctity of the family name. Most fell by the wayside, the life too rigorous or too coarse for their delicate sensibilities. The families were not always notified of the black sheep's departure from Australia feet first. It was Nick's observation that no news was good news in such cases.

"Where would you have gone?" Nick asked casually, but far more interested than he wanted Slayton to know at present.

"America."

"Anything different about your story from most idiotic tales of youthful excess?" Nick's voice dripped acid. He had no use for young wastrels. He'd never had a youth to squander. It was grinding work or starvation where he came from.

"No different."

Nick liked that. Charlie Slayton was a sinner, but not a puling baby. A plan was forming, but Nick wasn't going to save Charlie from himself unless he passed a few more hurdles.

"My name's Nicholas Monroe," Nick said, handing over his flask again. "What have you done with yourself all these years?"

"Nothing notable. I wanted to go into the army, but the family chose the church for me," Slayton said, the first edge of bitterness showing. "I'm a lot of things, none of which fit me for the pulpit. I didn't want to be a huntin'-and-shootin' vicar either. It wouldn't have been fair to the people who believe."

Charlie Slayton passed another test. He was brutally honest with himself.

They drove at a leisurely pace for miles, unwilling or unable to summon the energy or interest to exchange life histories. They passed villages and hamlets bedded down for the night, seemingly unmoved by the clean, cool air, the lowing of animals, the occasional yelping dog marking their passage to London.

The first light of dawn and they were approaching the outskirts of London before they spoke again.

"How's the leg?"

"Hellish."

"Where shall I drop you?"

"In the Thames."

"That's the end of the drink talking."

"Look, sir, why are you letting me off so lightly?" Charlie turned, his young/old face gray with fatigue and his eyes bloodshot and red-rimmed. "I did an awful thing, and it was only God's misplaced mercy that you didn't decapitate or shoot me."

Charlie Slayton could not have said anything more to win his case.

"Where do you live?"

"At the Albany," Charlie said proudly, revealing the first sign of haughtiness.

"And what the hell is the Albany?" Nick asked, the first disappointment in Charlie and a momentary setback in the fanciful plans he had been mulling all through the curious night.

Charlie sensed Nick's retreat. He moved cautiously, trying to detect what he had said that would have offended his unlikely savior.

"Have you been in London long, sir?"

"Nearer to fourteen days. Why?"

"Any man with social pretensions in London for making a name for himself among the bucks would give his right arm for such an address. I have a bad habit of crowing over my good fortune in having chambers at the Albany."

At once Charlie Slayton shot himself in the foot again. He felt Nick stiffen beside him. Obviously it was the wrong answer by far. The Arctic freeze he felt coming from the other side of the carriage confirmed it.

"Look, Mr. Monroe, what have I said to distress you—and don't tell me I haven't," Charlie insisted, holding his breath.

During the long, silent night Slayton had become interested, and then intrigued, about the curious man next to him and by the way matters had fallen out. Monroe had delivered him from perhaps the most colossal of all his stupid escapades. His disgust with his continued failures to be the man he'd started to be was monumental, and for the first time in his life Lord Charles Slayton, the third and last son of the Earl of Ballyor, felt that only a miracle could save him.

When the full meaning of what might have happened on the road the night before dawned on him during the long night's ride, Charlie very nearly took the gun Monroe had returned to him and put a period to his useless life. His hand had gone to the pistol several times, but each time he withdrew.

Why hadn't he killed himself? He had no fear of hell. He'd found it at every turn the last year. That it was the coward's way out didn't wash with Charlie. Instead, he began to believe the man next to him was the reason he was still alive. From the first moment, Charlie, despite his drunken haze, sensed that Monroe was no ordinary man. He didn't need to know anything about Nick's past or read his face to feel his strength and goodness.

Charlie turned to look at Nick's now rigid profile, realizing he must have put his foot in it by talking so snobbishly about the Albany, and he was sorry. Charlie's charm—only he didn't know it—was his irrepressible optimism, which took sway again. It was this that kept him at the card tables when his luck was out. The errant instinct that made him bet everything he owned or ever hoped to own on each improbable high-jinx, get-rich-quick scheme, made him wake every morning with high expectations that this was the day when his fortunes would change. Could meeting the big Australian, who kept him from making the biggest of all mistakes of his wasted life, turn the tide? Charlie wasn't often fanciful, but he felt instantly drawn to the man next to him.

"I owe you my life, Mr. Monroe," Charlie said, hoping he could find the words to bridge the chasm that had opened between them. Not even the holdup had seemed to rattle Monroe as much as a few thoughtless words. "I feel I've just made a terrible mistake, and I would deem it a courtesy if you would tell me what I said to offend you."

Nick slowed the horses and extracted a cigar from an inside pocket. To tell Charlie what was bothering him sounded in his ears churlish and worse, unmanly. Nick felt a warm flush erupt in the pit of his stomach. He would have died if any of his Australian mates knew he had spent the night plotting to make use of Charlie Slayton for his own ambitions formed the night at the rickety theater.

"Sod it," Nick said angrily, throwing his cigar to the side of the road and picking up the horses' pace.

"Now what the deuce have I done to make you angry again?" Charlie yelled over the noise of the galloping horses.

"Forget it. Just tell me where that bloody Albany is."

Charlie was still puzzled. Would Monroe give him a second chance? They rode in silence, coming to Hyde Park at last, where Charlie proceeded to point the way. He made quick adjustments to his torn and dusty clothes, checked the state of his tall hat, and drew a handkerchief quickly over his face in preparation for their arrival. It wouldn't do for Albany servants to see him disheveled in the early morning. They were a cavalry of magpies, and word of his latest contretemps would sweep through the venerable old house like an ill wind and no doubt get back to his father's valet by evening. He sighed audibly, his spirits even lower than before. Would he never stop plaguing his poor father?

Nick noticed the repairs the man was trying to make to his appearance and wondered why Slayton bothered about how he looked, unless it was another one of the confounded secrets of a London gentleman which were still a mystery to him. No upstanding Australian cared a fig for the way he looked, or, if he did, would never dream of making a display of it in front of another bloke.

The late-morning traffic was a mad tangle of carts, riders, and carriages moving at a snail's pace. Nick was relieved when his companion pointed to two imposing stone lodges on either side of a large courtyard. Nick had passed the house with awe many times in his wanderings about the town.

"You live here?" Nick asked, incredulous at the size and grandeur of the mansion set back from busy Piccadilly. No wonder Charlie boasted of his lodgings.

Nick's curricle made a smart entry in and around the spacious yard with stables flanking each side, teeming with carriages of all sizes and ready hands already at work.

"My father has had rooms here since Henry Holland turned the place into sets of chambers for gentlemen," Charlie said, treading carefully. He didn't want to offend Monroe again.

"How does one acquire a set of chambers, or whatever you called them?"

Nick could see himself ensconced in the Albany on the first step of his much-amended master design. The thought of going back to his dingy hotel weighed on him like a rock.

"The Albany has a list of hopefuls who have waited for years," Charlie said warily, afraid of committing another gaffe. "These rooms are part of one's patrimony. No gentleman gives up such luxury in the heart of the town."

"There has to be a way around it," Nick muttered, determined he was not going to be thwarted. His admiration for the noble building deepened. The double doors of the house were open, and he saw an arresting view down a paneled hall. At the end was a peaked roof over a path lined with two-story buildings. He had an irresistible urge to examine the place for himself.

No longer anxious to see the last of Charlie Slayton, Nick was torn by curiosity, and ordered the servants who came to help out of his way. He came around the curricle quickly and swung Slayton over his shoulder like a sack of potatoes.

"You can lead the way now, lads," Nick called out, fairly bounding up the front steps, with the liveried servants hurrying before them to the end of the hall and Charlie's chambers.

"Mr. Monroe, this isn't really necessary," Charlie protested, the spectacle of being carried by Nick too mortifying.

"Lord Charles, are you in need of a doctor?" a valet who opened the large double door of the flat exclaimed, rushing to take his master from Nick's shoulder.

"Not at all," Nick said, dumping Charlie on a couch. "Nothing's broken. Needs a bit of ice water and some wrappings, and he'll be right as rain."

Nick delivered his diagnosis while surveying the size and furnishings of the opulent, high-ceilinged drawing room, sunlight coming through the huge bowed windows overlooking the Italian garden that separated the great house and the low buildings beyond.

Charlie laughed. Monroe's ill-concealed admiration of the room reminded him of the last pair of bailiffs who had gloated over their luck in finding such an Aladdin's treasure. They thought to empty all the rooms of their ancient Gobelin tapestries, Turkish carpets, and other rich adornments, only to find that everything belonged to Charlie's father.

"I would gladly share all this with you," Charlie said, his arms sweeping the magnificent room and its opulent furnishings.

Nick didn't reply until he circled the room.

"What I want, I can't buy, and that's where you come in, Lord Charles Bloody Slayton."

"Sorry about that, old man, I prefer to forget my title when I'm behaving like a fool," Charlie admitted, blushing like a schoolboy.

Once more, Nick found Charlie's honesty difficult to resist, and his anger abated.

"Some breakfast, Mr. Monroe?" Charlie asked, sensing the mood change and remembering his manners and all he owed his deliverer.

Nick's first thought was to refuse, but he quickly changed his mind. Returning to his cell at the hotel was too daunting, and this room too inviting to leave so quickly. He nodded, and Charlie ordered Stevens, his valet, to prepare the meal with all haste.

Nick resumed his examination of the luxurious room. "Tell me who painted those pictures," Nick asked, his eyes riveted on two paintings on a far wall.

"That's a Turner landscape; the other a Van Dyck portrait of an ancestor," Charlie answered simply.

Silver, gilt, and enamel ornaments of uncommon beauty made Nick's hands itch to touch. He had always wanted to be surrounded by art and music and beauty of every description, and now here was his chance. He would own such perfection of form and execution, he told himself. Clearly Charlie appreciated and knew what was exceptional. For while Nick might not know perfect Meissen from other porcelain, he knew what he liked, and that, according to his mother, who knew about fine possessions, was half the battle. "Taste first; second money," was one of her maxims.

Charlie observed his rescuer without giving any sign he was doing so, touched to the core to see Nick soften, his eyes warm, with a kind of hunger and admiration for the contents of the room.

"Tell me, Slayton, do you know a lot about all this?" Nick asked, his hand indicating the richness of the decorations.

Nick meant to be casual in his question, but in fact he was holding his breath. What he saw surrounding him was what he wanted in his own life in London and Delacourt House.

"If I may be permitted to boast," Charlie said, laughing, "my mother was quite an authority on art and furniture, and as the only one of the family who shared it, we haunted the auction rooms and artists' studios. She said I had a natural eye."

In two strides, Nick Monroe was across the room.

"Would you teach me all you know?"

Chapter Five

The weather continued fair, and Kate prodded her maid, who was given to gawking at the shop windows and butcher boys who eyed her as eagerly as she eyed them.

At the best of times, Kate's long steps were a trial to the young servant, newly arrived in London. But when her ladyship was as lighthearted as she seemed the last week, there was no stopping her gallivanting about the town like a demented hare.

Kate's mood had lightened considerably since Barbara Maitland and Colby Browning had rescued her from Peterbroome at the Holland's ball. They had taken it into their beautiful collective heads to interest themselves in the younger woman as never before. Kate was still unaware how desperate and plaintive she sounded when she said good-bye to her friends that dawn, and since then they had kept her busy with one charitable mission after another.

"The girl's moldering in front of our eyes, and we are letting it happen without lifting a finger," Colby said in her hyperbolic way, carrying the cooler Barbara along with her.

"I do believe, dear Colby, you are the only human being in all of London who would dare suggest that the radiant, incomparable Kate, who has never been in better looks, is moldering," Barbara said, laughing.

"She did say she was drowning, after all," Colby countered.

Today a happier Kate Grovenor was hurrying into Bond Street later than she wanted. She had no desire to be seen there after the noon hour, when the usual Regency loungers would have left their beds to parade along the crowded street to see and be seen in the latest fashions decreed acceptable by Beau Brummell and his imitators and disciples.

Kate was almost a yard ahead of her servant when she entered Bond Street at last, heading for the Western Exchange, the splendid new bazaar in the rear of the Burlington Arcade. Her task was to beg and cajole contributions for various charitable sales Barbara and Colby were holding during the season.

She doubted her friends' claim that her name and face were all that was needed to insure a profitable expedition. She found they were right. After an hour Kate and her hapless maid were walking through the arcade to Piccadilly, each weighed down with beribboned bandboxes and laughing like schoolgirls, when they collided with two men sauntering past.

In the confusion that followed, Kate's pretty chip hat was knocked askew, and when she could right it, the shorter and younger of the two men recognized her, lowering her dignity even further.

"Darling Kate, how wonderful." Charlie Slayton took her in his arms and hugged her, sending her few remaining packages sailing every which way.

Kate was impressed with her cousin's striking appearance, blond and slim, his face lean, his eyes clear. For once there were few signs of past dissipation. She was so absorbed in studying the change in Charlie and retrieving her packages, that she hardly noticed the man towering beside her.

Nick was thunderstruck.

The Lady in Gray! He couldn't believe his luck.

Nick was grateful for the spare moment to recover his balance, dangerously overset in the discovery that Charlie not only knew his mystery lady, but was holding her in his arms. His grand scheme was once again knocked sideways by this woman. He had hoped for more time to smooth his rough edges before they met again. His senses vibrated like an aspen tree, and Nick took the few seconds allotted him by the collison to take in everything about her, hoping at closer range to find she had a deforming squint or blemish of some kind, anything that would shake the pedestal he had installed her on in his dreams. But no, she was flesh and blood real, unmarred, unmarked, and as magnificent as she had been on stage when she first poleaxed him a month before.

"Charlie, you're looking fabulously well," Kate exclaimed in her throaty voice, looking him up and down, puzzled by the obvious changes in him. "Everyone's been asking what happened to you."

Slayton blushed. "Ah, my manners, dear Kate," Slayton said, not sure how much he should say in front of Nick.

"May I introduce to you my very new friend, Mr. Nicholas Monroe, late of Australia, a new resident and an ardent admirer of our beloved city," Charlie said enthusiastically, playing for time. "Nick, this is my favorite relative, Lady Katherine Grovenor."

Barely aware of Nick until that moment, she pivoted and was momentarily struck dumb by the height and breadth of the man, but more so by dark, warmly smiling eyes in a startlingly handsome, tanned face.

Nick groaned silently. His cause was lost. His Lady in Gray was, in fact, a member of the nobility, and not a courtesan as he'd come to hope. And why not? Wasn't she all he'd imagined an aristocratic Englishwoman would be—elegant, lovely, and kind? In the sweetly tormented nights after he'd seen her leave the theater, he'd hoped she was some peer's fancy piece. At least then he would have had a chance to vie for her attention. Now he hadn't a prayer in hell. A peer's daughter was another matter entirely and far above the touch of a roughneck foreigner.

Nick bowed and kissed the proffered hand. His heart was beating in what was becoming an all too familiar tattoo, and he prayed he was the only one to hear it. If ever the Fates smiled on him, he wanted it to be now. Nick's fear of putting a foot wrong made his throat as dry as the Sahara, his tongue tied in knots. He was happy to settle for Kate to ignore him until he could recoup his bearings.

The last thing he wanted to do was make an ass of him-

self in front of Kate, of all people. He bowed and reluctantly released her hand.

Kate smiled, trying to remember where she had seen
Charlie's friend before. Nicholas Monroe was hardly someone one could easily overlook or forget, and she dismissed
the feeling as quickly as it came.

"Charlie, now tell me why you look so different," she
asked, and then, studying Charlie closer, felt she knew.
"You have been rusticating in the country. And what a very
great thing that is."

"Actually, my darling girl, I have almost not bestirred
myself from the Albany, and if I look quite the thing, you
can lay it at the door of Mr. Monroe," Slayton said. It was
time someone knew how much he owed Nick. The whole
truth was too shaming, of course, but that didn't mean he
couldn't give credit where it belonged and where it would
do Nick the most good.

Kate turned to look inquiringly at the large figure beside
her. Something in the way Charlie, the most ironic and cynical of men, looked at his newfound friend, made Kate want
to study him closely. From the start the Australian radiated
strength and assurance, but now she saw more. He had the
most generous mouth and the kindest dark eyes, and she
felt drawn to the man far more than was sensible on such
short acquaintance. She felt shy suddenly, and couldn't understand it.

Kate wasn't at all certain that she liked the way Nicholas
Monroe made her feel. It was a new experience to find herself drawn to someone she barely knew, especially a complete stranger. The most expert of London's cadre of
practiced dandies had tried to engage her interest and turn
her head, yet here was someone who barely acknowledged
her existence, so unexceptional was his greeting to her. Yet
she could think of nothing to say, captivated as she was by
his quiet strength and Adonis physique. Was she in danger
of losing her poise to a colonial just because he was big and
commanding? Wasn't she immune to such things? How absurd.

Still, she must remember her manners, and if he had really been instrumental in helping to restore some luster to Charlie's tarnished career, she was grateful.

"Now what could you possibly have done to our sadly loose fish to make him so high in his praise of you and look fairly ten years younger, my dear sir?" Kate asked saucily. For, indeed, it was an age since Charlie had looked clear-eyed and full of life as he did that day.

"My dear Lady Katherine, it is I who have to thank Charlie, for he has set out to make a gentleman of me overnight, and I doubt that I am an apt pupil."

Nick was throwing caution to the wind, admitting his humble origins and his ambitions unashamedly. He couldn't blame her if she laughed at him, but something, quite outside himself, made him reckless. It was a strange path he had chosen, a gamble in fact, but he didn't care.

"That is not precisely true." Charlie jumped in quickly, afraid Nick would say too much and shock Kate and her aristocratic prejudices. "Nick's a gentleman to his finger-tips, and all I am doing is helping him acquire a little town bronze."

Nick understood at once that Charlie was signaling him to keep his too Australian honesty to himself, but he never wanted to pass under false colors, least of all to this be-witching woman.

"Charlie's trying to put a good face on it, but I am, after all, a newborn babe by London standards, and I will not fly under anyone's flag but my own," Nick said firmly. "I wish to live well and comfortably and to know my way about properly."

Kate stood openmouthed listening to them. She was so touched by the big man's rigid code and Charlie's attempt to protect Monroe from himself, that she didn't know where to turn. She felt inexplicably drawn to Nicholas Monroe, who was such an original after all the poseurs and fools who littered her life. And she wanted to laugh be-cause Charlie, of all people, who had broken every known law of gentlemanly behavior, was quick to save his friend's reputation. What a pair!

The turnabout in her dissolute cousin was so obvious that

she was sure Charlie was on the road to redemption. And this rare man he had in tow was to be applauded for his efforts. Kate had long since relinquished her dimly lit Diogenes lantern in search of men of character and purpose in her brittle choice, and here today she met two extraordinary men. It was her lucky day.

"I want to be part of this," Kate said, grasping an arm of each man. "May I join forces with you today after I rid myself of my booty?"

Nick couldn't believe he'd heard aright. Not only had she not taken a disgust of him, which Charlie must have feared she would, but she was eager and genuinely pleased about their scheme. Nick quickly propelled Kate's maid toward the Albany to dispose of Kate's boxes. He didn't want to lose a moment with his mystery woman.

Slayton took Kate aside. "Be sure this isn't some kind of cruel whim," Charlie warned her. "The man saved my life, paid some of my more pressing debts, and is the salt of the earth. I shall throttle anyone who hurts him, and that includes you, dear cousin."

Kate was struck by Charlie's vehemence. Was it a whim on her part, a chance to kick over the traces and have some innocent fun? Perhaps it started that way, but if Monroe meant that much to Charlie, and Monroe was everything she suspected, she would move heaven and earth to help the Australian have his wish. It was the least she could do for Charlie, her ally against the world since they were children.

"Tell me, what can I do?" Kate asked.

"There seems to be a woman he loves, but she's far above him, at least that is what he says."

"Who is she?" Kate asked.

"Haven't a clue. But I am persuaded all this haste to be a proper London gent is in aid of being worthy of her," Charlie said. "He isn't interested in meeting other women. He's told me quite definitely he's never been in love before. Obviously, he is over the moon about this woman."

Kate was at a loss to know why the idea of turning Nicholas Monroe into a proper Regency buck seemed less exciting than at first. What had started, she realized now, as a pleasant diversion, was less so. Kate shrugged off the sudden onslaught of doubt about the fun she had anticipated. She was committed, and she would do it with her whole heart, as she did everything, but something seemed missing from her earlier enthusiasm.

Nick and Kate's maid returned to them. "Where do we begin?"

"Clothes to start with," Kate said, surveying the long out-of-fashion greatcoat, worn beaver hat, and ugly, bulky boots.

"Weston of Bond Street it shall be," Charlie said delightedly.

"No. We are taking him to Abraham Ellis of St. James's Street," Kate said, pulling them along Piccadilly. "Tarn Maitland and Nevil Browning have given him their custom, and he will soon supplant Weston. He is all the crack."

"Right you are, my dear coz," Charlie said.

"With Lobb's for boots and Locke's for hats down the street, we shall have you looking like a toff, Mr. Monroe," Kate said gaily.

"I say, is all this comme il faut?" Nick asked, halting in midstep. "Do woman accompany men to such shopping expeditions?"

At once Charlie's face fell. Kate's father was a high stickler for form, although a reprobate himself, and Charlie wanted no trouble from that quarter. His granduncle Grovenor was a difficult man, as he had cause to know.

"I have never done it before, but it would seem to me what's good for the goose, and all that rot," Kate said, determinedly moving toward the shops on the busy thoroughfare. In for a penny, in for a pound. She was sick of accommodating the narrow constraints placed on women in society. "Men have accompanied me for ribbons and books. They are thick on the ground at modistes. Why is my shopping with you and Mr. Monroe so far out of the common way?"

"Kate, we are going to be buying smallclothes and such.

Perhaps Nick's instincts are better than ours," Charlie said, mulishly.

"Let's chance it," Kate insisted. "I shall only attend you as far as the selection of materials for coats and proceed to choose leather at Lobb's for Mr. Monroe's boots and hats at Locke's while you finish at the tailor."

The compromise was accepted, albeit warily on Charlie's part. The whirlwind created by the trio in the three shops lasted two hours amid much laughter and expense.

Exhausted, and in great pleasure with one another, they appeared at Gunther's for a late lunch. Kate and Charlie greeted friends and acquaintances, introducing Nick to all and sundry. Thereafter, they were lost to the stares and murmurings caused by their high good spirits and their interest in each other.

Of the trio, Kate was the first to sense that Nick was causing great and noisy interest. Her keen awareness of atmosphere told her that the feverish whispering was probably brought on by the foreignness of his clothes and startlingly Greek-god looks. Everything about Nick Monroe marked him as a stranger or, worse, an alien. Kate was offended for this kind and enchanting man who had captured her imagination in just a few hours. She was well aware of the English resentment against anyone not born and bred in the kingdom, especially anyone who didn't speak or dress like the rest of the *ton*.

It was not one of the finer characteristics of her countrymen, and she was embarrassed by their prejudices. And ashamed, too. Had she in the past been as insulated and intolerant of differences in other people? She hoped not. If nothing else, this day would be memorable, for henceforth she resolved she would monitor her behavior toward others far more carefully than she had ever dreamed of doing in the past.

Without realizing it, Kate put a hand on Nick's coat sleeve, feeling at once protective, knowing it would take all hers and Charlie's considerable social cachet to introduce Nick Monroe to society successfully. But if that was what this good and kind man wanted, between them they would bring it about. The covert career on stage she pursued was done precisely to get her away from the superficial life of the people he seemed anxious to know. There was no accounting for taste, Kate concluded.

Across the table, it took all of Nick's self-control to keep from staring and feasting at the long, slim fingers resting on his sleeve and covering them with his own. He longed for the feel of her, the longing making him tremble with naked desire. The short time he'd spent with Kate this day was his first glimpse of heaven, and he would no nothing to spoil it. But the effort was almost more than he could bear. These two delightful, unself-conscious, warm, and generous people more than made up for the weeks he'd been meant to feel the rankest outsider.

"I don't believe I have thanked you properly," Nick started to say, putting his hands in his lap lest they see how truly shaken he was by the events of the day. "I thought London was the most inhospitable place on earth until I met you."

This encouraged Charlie to tell Kate some of the things that had befallen Nick before he had met him, carefully editing his own contribution to the sorry story.

"He had a terrible experience in a villain's tavern he wandered into innocently." Charlie proceeded to tell her what happened.

"Aren't all taverns the same?" Kate asked, appalled by the story.

"In many respects the worst gin mill and criminal's crib is like the most inaccessible St. James gentlemen's club," Charlie explained patiently. "People want only to be with their own sort. That will never change. An Englishman's drink house is almost more sacred than his home. Strangers are not invited or wanted."

"Yes, of course, Charlie, but why not tell Mr. Monroe the whole of it," Kate said harshly. "He's a foreigner, and Englishmen prize the Channel and the isolation it gives them."

Charlie agreed, though he'd never examined the possibility before.

Nick sensed that conversation had stopped around them. He was not unmindful of the interest his presence had created in these fashionable surroundings in the beginning, and supposed it was starting to pall. He guessed his clothes marked him for what he was. A feeling of gloom and disappointment invaded his spirit. He'd talked himself into believing that people would take him at more than face value; that he could win acceptance with his character and ambition. How raw, how young he was. He felt the other patrons' first interest in him turn into disapproval. Well, the hell with pretense and their scorn.

"I am an Australian, actually born here, but nevertheless a colonial, and worse, from a colony of criminals," Nick said. "Have you any idea how beastly your government keepers treat the poor souls whom they transport and forget about?"

Nick's voice had risen. He had their attention. If these pampered English wanted an earful, he would give it to them.

"The horrors of the slave trade which everyone knows about are sometimes more merciful compared to transportation. The butchery and inhumanity shown toward the prisoners begins on the ships," Nick said, remembering his own experiences and all he'd heard. "On one ship alone, of the 499 on board, only 72 landed in fair health. One man had 10,000 lice on him, and he lay in the irons the whole miserable journey, unable to do more than moan and cry."

He barely paused for breath. "Even when masters are paid bonuses for healthy prisoners, many are just as sadistic as before. They starve the people and sell the supplies they have been given to feed him to settlers, who wait for them on arrival in Sydney Cove."

Nick paused and drank his tea. "And it's no Eden on land. It is the death of hope. Convicts, many of whom are no better than they should be, still do not deserve to be treated worse than work animals, less so in most cases. They are starved and lashed to work longer than the beasts. Many die horrible deaths from beatings. No one cares.

Labor is cheap, and another man waits to fill the dead man's shoes."

Nick was pale and shaking, but he wasn't finished.

"And for what? The real crime behind the original conception of transportation was the official reason you don't know. It was less to punish convicts, and more to wipe out all criminals in this country," he said between clenched teeth. "The final joke is that crime is greater than ever in England, isn't it?"

The unrelieved brutality of Nick's revelations told Kate, if not Charlie, that what they were hearing was not just hearsay, but personal and firsthand. She felt an uncommon bond building for this man who must have suffered great hurt, the kind her imagination and sympathy could not encompass.

Kate felt shamed and inadequate to the task of alleviating the misery she saw on Nick's face. What succor could she give him? Cocooned by birth and money, what could she know of the suffering Nick described?

"If I do nothing else with my money, I shall try to right a few of the wrongs, especially for the families torn apart by government indifference," Nick said, afraid he sounded like a politician, a breed he could not abide.

"On that score, Mr. Monroe, Charlie and I may be able to assist you. We can arrange an introduction to Captain Tarn Maitland, a most influential friend, whose heart is easily touched," Kate said, feeling at once relieved that she could do something for Nick. Her own charities amounted to seeing to the welfare of her father's tenants and nearby villagers neglected by him. Her support of Herr Hendricks's band of players seemed pitifully inadequate when set beside Nicholas Monroe's mission.

Again, Kate put her arm on Nick's sleeve, giving him her silent support.

This time Nick didn't hesitate to put his hand over hers. He knew it would be the first and only time he would be able to do so. Even if she had not taken a disgust of him for his outburst, Nick knew, better than she, the deep gulf that divided them could never be bridged. He was the son of a convict, however innocent his father was of the charge.

In all his youthful yearnings, Nicholas had never included a desire to be a gentleman worthy of the hand of someone as exalted as Lady Katherine Grovenor. What could he be thinking? His ambitions forged years ago as a ragtag urchin in the back street hovels of Sydney were far more modest and reasonable. All he wanted then and when he landed in London was a chance to live well and make up to his mother all the lost years and hardships she had endured for love of Aden Monroe. Nick's aspirations for himself went no further than to live the life of a country squire, master of Delacourt House, sharing the estate with his mother. He wanted to see her as the chatelaine of a house she always loved and deserved to call her own.

But that seemed years ago and were the desires of a simpler man. How could he have known anyone like Kate Grovenor existed? When he thought about a wife, it was never a woman of such high rank. Yet here he was, hopelessly infatuated with Kate, who, for all her apparent goodness and interest in furthering his career, was a world apart, and would remain always beyond his grasp.

He'd lost his heart, but not his sense. He would remedy that lapse, and one day might look back on all this as an interlude, nothing more.

The thought of never seeing Kate Grovenor chilled him to the bone. He had to leave. She was like a magnet, and he was fast losing his way in those great green eyes.

Pleading a pressing appointment with Hooper, Nick begged to be excused and left Kate and Charlie at the table.

He meant to put his new resolve into practice at once. He would move out of Charlie's flat at the Albany and disappear from their lives as quietly as he came. Explanations for his sudden departure would be too painful. He couldn't tell them the truth. A guttersnipe would make a poor lord, and a lord would make a poor guttersnipe. He needed solitude and distance to recover from his wild flight from re-ality.

Nick's abrupt departure left the others feeling a heavy cloud had settled on them.

"Charlie, what is Mr. Monroe's history?" Kate asked when Nick was lost to sight. It seemed of the utmost moment that she learn all that was to be known about the man who had taken the sun with him when he left. Kate couldn't remember the last time her interest in a man had become so quickly engaged.

The stark truth was she never met Nick Monroe's like before. Encountering men of simple origins, who had become rich by their own endeavors, was a new experience for Kate. The one exception was Captain Tarn Maitland, who had made his mark and fortune as a daring sea captain years before. And she'd heard rumors that Maitland's father was a lord. Most men Kate knew were rich by birth or marriage, mostly in huge land holdings. Few had enhanced the wealth they inherited by dirtying their hands. Some she'd heard had been judicious in the management of their estates or the lease of the coal and tin and other minerals beneath their holdings. Few had started from disadvantage, as she suspected Nick did. For reasons she couldn't explain to herself, she wanted to know everything about Nick, and she wanted to know at once.

"I know less than nothing about Nick Monroe, although I think he was on the point of telling me several times during my confinement," Charlie said.

"Your what?"

"I have a rather disgraceful story to tell you," Slayton confessed, gathering up their packages and leading Kate to the street. If he was to tell her the whole sorry mess, he didn't want an audience of giggling misses and bluestocking dowagers knowing every sordid detail. He hurried her along the crowded streets toward her home, talking as fast as he walked, wanting her to know everything before his courage failed.

"The truth is, Nick moved into the Albany with me and helped me stay sober while my leg healed," Slayton said, winding up his story. "He stayed with me day and night while I climbed the walls backwards wanting a drink and made me give him a short university course in fine art, furniture, silver, and music. He was like a sponge and has the most unerring good taste, and, I daresay, in a few months will surpass me."

"Poor Charlie," Kate said, not sure whether to laugh or cry at the more hilarious parts of the midnight holdup, but appalled nevertheless by the reason for the foolhardy adventure.

"Why didn't you come to me for help?"

"Where were you going to get 15,000 pounds?" Slayton laughed hollowly.

"Your father or Papa."

"My father has written me off. Not another farthing. And your father may be among the warmest men in town, but he had been known to outdistance even his income," Charlie said bleakly. "From what I hear, Uncle Pearson has been most unfortunate in his plunges at the card table recently. He could hardly be persuaded to fund me. Besides, he hates me."

"Oh, Charlie, what are you going to do now?"

"You weren't listening, my dear girl. Monroe has paid off more than half my debts on condition that I give up gambling, carousing, and drinking for a year. I remain in his employ until I pay off the rest."

"All for introducing him to the *ton* for that lady of his?"

Charlie nodded. "I suppose. But I will need your help. Your consequence is far greater than mine, you know."

"Done." Kate didn't hesitate for a moment, adding pertly, "I can't imagine anything that would give me more pleasure. But you must truly allow me full part in Monroe's transformation. Although from what I can see he has more natural poise than most of our friends."

They had arrived at the door of Grovenor House, an imposing white mansion with black iron railings and balconies built to last at the express wish of the Regent. He liked his subjects to wave at him when he rode past their houses. Charlie turned and studied his cousin. "What have you in that agile mind of yours? And don't tell me you are not hatching something."

"To start with, I will write to Lady Givens and have you both invited to her costume party tonight," Kate said easily.

"And where will Nick get a costume to fit him at this hour?" Charlie protested.

"Don't worry. You'll find something for both of you."

"Kate, you're daft."

"Your papa has a wardrobe full of things, and they are of all sizes. Put that brain of yours to work."

"And why not?" Charlie answered, kissing her on the cheek. "You are a brick, and meeting you today was brilliant."

Kate watched him go, and entered the house, full of plans for furthering Nick Monroe's career.

The butler took Kate's coat and parasol and purposefully led her away from the front door. Kate was alarmed. Jenkins's manner was so insistent, his basset-hound face more hangdog than usual.

"Jenkins, what is it?"

"The master asked that you see him as soon as you returned."

At once Kate's mood of happy expectation lowered to cold concern. Her father was seldom home early in the day, and Jenkins, her friend, her buffer between her parents and confidant in the years of her lonely childhood, was never solemn with her.

"What troubles are brewing?" Kate asked breathlessly. Pearson Grovenor and most of the *ton* lived in the certainty that servants were deaf, dumb, and blind, and they rarely moderated their voices or their brains in front of retainers.

"He is in extreme perturbation, my lady," the man said fearfully. "He has had a visitor."

"Who was it?" Kate asked.

"I would rather not say, but his lordship is in a state, if I may say so. I advise you to be very careful."

Chapter Six

"Peterbroome. You can't be serious." Kate's voice shook with outrage.

"He wants your hand in marriage, and I have agreed."

"No!" Kate shouted.

"It's time you settled down, and Peterbroome is as good as anyone."

"The worst."

"He said you would not like it," her father said with sardonic satisfaction.

"You know we detest each other, and have since childhood."

"He wants you now. I warned him you wouldn't suit, but he is a determined man and gets what he wants."

"I will not have him, Papa, and that is the end of it." Kate knew this was not the way to her father's heart, in the remote possibility that he had one, but she didn't care. Anything, anyone, but not Peterbroome.

Pearson Grovenor rose in mighty rage, knocking his chair backward with a crash.

"How dare you presume to tell me whom you will and will not have once I have given my word?" His tone was glacial. "I have arranged a union between two of England's first families. You should be on your knees thanking me."

"Papa, please," Kate begged, trying to recoup some of the ground she had lost with her unwise outburst.

"I need this, and nothing you say or do will alter my decision." Her father turned his back on her and moved to the drinks table.

"I don't understand. What can you mean when you say you need this marriage?"

"That is not your concern," he said, pouring himself a generous tot of madeira, his hands shaking.

"Surely you are not under the hatches?" Kate remembered Charlie Slayton telling her about her father's losses at the tables. "Surely, of all people, you don't have to sell a daughter to the highest bidder and one of the most depraved men in London."

Grovenor turned, his bloodshot eyes smoldering, knocking his glass against the table, the liquid running down his biscuit-colored breeches.

"What have you heard?" He crossed the room to stand menacingly over her, his voice demanding. "Tell me."

"I have heard nothing," Kate murmured, backing away from the fury that contorted his once handsome face.

Kate guessed there was more to this grotesque betrothal than Grovenor pride of family, which was, in fact, dearer to her father than anything under the sun, including her. Kate couldn't envision what hold Peterbroome had over him, but whatever it was it must be something considerable.

Why hadn't she listened to the butler's warning? Why hadn't she bridled her tongue? She knew she could never prevail in any contest of wills with this man she hated. Hated. Admitting her true feelings for her father, hidden even from herself since she was a child, was, if possible, even more devastating than her betrothal to Peterbroome.

Kate moved blindly to a settee near the window. She needed to recover her wits. You're an actress. Think of something, she told herself. Kate took a deep breath, making the effort loud enough to draw her father's attention.

"Papa, must I give you my answer now?" Kate asked in a small voice, giving the reading just enough pathos to thaw even someone as callous as her father, while it sickened her.

"He is not a patient man," Grovenor replied with a malicious grin. "He said you wouldn't like him for a husband. Said I've spoiled you rotten letting you run wild. He'll tame you."

Kate bit back a bitter reply. Her future husband's way of taming a woman was an open secret among both his friends and enemies, of which he had more of the latter than the former. Kate tried to still the beating of her heart. It wouldn't do to show her father her fears again. It was enough that she knew what she could expect in a life with a practiced sadist and satyr. Her father knew Peterbroome's reputation far better than she could, and yet he was willing to sell her to the worst roué for reasons of his own.

That Peterbroome held power over her father was no longer in doubt. All she could see was a yawning pit beneath her feet. The combination of her father and Peterbroome was too much for her. Kate once thought she could never be defeated, but that was long before her father and Peterbroome were ranged against her. She had no one to turn to, and, what was worse, she didn't have money of her own. What little her mother left her she spent on Herr Hendricks and his troupe.

Who could she turn to who would dare take her in, take her part against her father? What she needed was a miracle, and Kate knew miracles were for dreamers. She rose from the chair and straightened her shoulders.

"I ask for a month to consider, Papa. No announcement until then."

"I never thought to see you missish, Kate. You knew the day would come when you would have to marry," her father growled. "You should be pleased. I have assured your future. All right, but not a moment more than a month, and that I will tell Peterbroome tonight."

Kate turned to leave the room. "A month can't matter to either of you."

"Nonsense," her father said, grown weary with arguing. He had achieved his goal: the family honor preserved, his recalcitrant daughter tamed. What matter whom a woman was shackled to? He didn't hold with cosseting females, never did and never would. He admitted grudgingly that only his natural indolence had kept him from exerting himself to see his incomparable daughter comfortably fixed. As it turned out, it was just as well that he hadn't married her off before.

Without Kate, that worm Peterbroome would have ruined him. But with her as his last remaining counter, he had something powerful to bargain with. Pearson Grovenor knew he would miss the attention of all the young swains who sought to curry favor with him as a means of pushing their suit with Kate. It had been lovely sport to play the suitors off against each other and to watch his cronies, whose daughters were dead fish in the annual Marriage Market, envy him for having given life to such a beauty.

Grovenor became aware that Kate stood before him, her normal radiance subdued, and the sense of power it gave him was heady. Until Peterbroome had finally proposed the marriage to settle the matter between then, he had felt weak and ineffectual. Now all would be as before, and that was enough to be getting on with.

"I expect you by my side tonight, and don't play the dying swan. Is that clear?"

All the fight had gone out of Kate. Lost to caring, she quit the room. All she knew was that she had a reprieve.

Maybe the world would end in a month.

Chapter Seven

"Iam going as an American Indian, and this is for you."
Charlie held up a richly frogged Cossack's uniform with
braid and buttons, large and resplendent enough to show off
Nick's enviable physique.

Charlie was so caught up in his triumph that it took a few
moments to see that Nick was packing.

"What is this?" Charlie was aghast. The thought that he
would not have Nick at his side, bolstering his new way of
life, was unthinkable. The man's company had become es-
sential to him, far exceeding Nick's generosity and care of
him. Charlie felt less need of drink and the excitement of
gambling and other riotous acts when he was with his
friend. Abstaining from his former life had been far less
difficult than he had ever dared consider. He actually liked
being sober and upright and learning about Nick's business
affairs.

"I ransacked my father's house to find this," Charlie
said, hoping Nick would offer a reasonable explanation
without prying. He knew the Australian was an intensely
private man and not one to talk about himself easily.

"Hooper rented a house in South Audley Street for me.
When my mother arrives, we can choose another dwelling,"
Nick said, willing Slayton to accept the explanation without
argument. Leaving irrepressible Charlie, the luxury, the
comforts, and collegiality shared with the other young Albany inhabitants Charlie had introduced him to would be a
great loss. He had quickly taken to the London bachelor
life, perhaps too quickly and too well. It was like having
the youth he never had in his pursuit of gold.

"Please, Nick, wait," Charlie pleaded. "Kate is securing invitations for us to the most important event of the week. If your education is to prosper, you must make an appearance with your sponsors at such well-attended parties."

Nick couldn't forgo a chance to see Kate Grovenor again.

"I will attend, but is it not asking Lady Katherine too much to include me, a foreign nobody, in her party?"

Charlie extracted a cigar from his case and sat down in a chair opposite the armoire that Nick continued emptying. He never fancied himself particularly sensitive, but Nick's company over the past weeks had given him some insights into the man and a desire to emulate him. The life of a rip and rousing blade had palled on him.

"Is this foreignness of yours going to be a raging hobby-horse? If it is, you will rapidly become impossible," Charlie said, sounding far more nonchalant than he felt. Charlie knew he was risking a fierce setdown, but his affection for Nick and a sixth sense told him he owed his mentor more than easy words and platitudes. An overexercised chip on Nick's shoulder would serve him ill in smart London circles.

"And what the hell does that mean, my fine lad?" Nick wheeled around, his eyes blazing. "You rich British make me sick. Your greatest fear is that the world's unpleasantness might intrude on your pleasures, and you must have fresh excitements at every moment."

The validity of the denunciation wasn't lost on Charlie. He was often appalled at the superficiality of his pleasure-mad friends. Still, if Nick spouted his feelings too often in public, it would not aid him in his efforts to make Nick an acceptable gentleman, and that for the moment was his prime concern. As he told Kate, he could only guess at the depths of the hurt that had colored Nick's life and made him the strong personality he was. Charlie thought himself as cynical as the next man, but at no time did he question that Nick Monroe was the salt of the earth. He knew in his bones that the big Australian was a man of character he could safely introduce to society without a qualm. Charlie knew too many bounders not to recognize one easily. No. Nick was an honorable man in every way as far as he could tell. Hadn't Nick spared his life and then turned into a friend ready to save him without a moment's hesitation? Charlie would have given a monkey to know what his history was, but knew Nick would divulge it in his own good time. He could wait.

"By God, you are a snob, Nick, old man," Charlie said after a while. "You are probably right in your estimate of me and my set, but if you want to live with your mother in peace here, then don't rail against us. Do something about it."

"I suppose I am becoming a bore," Nick conceded, taking the Cossack uniform from Charlie.

"I am quite sure that Tarn Maitland will be at the party tonight with Lord Nevil Browning, and Kate and I will introduce you," Charlie said reasonably, happy he had been able to reach Nick after all. "Then you can be inside the tent instead of pissing at us from without. They are reformers, and will welcome your tirades, even if I don't."

Nick smiled sheepishly. Charlie had given him the excuse he needed to salve his tender conscience, for he was pining to see Kate again. The hours since he left her at Gunther's so abruptly were bleak, and it might be the last time he saw her. He needed more time to give her up in his mind and, yes, in his body.

Kate's tears were long since spilled. Her future loomed dark and forbidding, and no amount of repining for what might have been had she accepted any of the scores of decent men who had wanted to marry her in the past could help her cause now. She was good and truly trapped, and she had no one to blame but herself.

Kate sat still as stone while her maid labored to tame her long titian hair into a fashion suitable for her Marie Antoinette costume. What to do about the heavy eyelids swollen from an hour's weeping exercised the young maid's considerable talents.

With a properly downcast look, the other guests will

think I am imagining myself on the way to the guillotine, which, after all, is the truth, Kate told herself grimly. If I am indeed the actress Herr Hendricks tells me I am, I shall carry off this role of a hapless queen in style. I might as well learn to act in life as well as on stage.

Kate looked for all the world every inch the queen when she joined her father later at the front door.

Jenkins smiled consolingly before draping the magnificent mantle matching her silver lace dress across her shoulders. Kate guessed the old retainer already knew before she did what life held in store for her.

"Well, my dear," her father said, openly admiring the way Kate looked, "I see you have accepted the inevitable. You are a Grovenor through and through."

It was the highest praise he could bestow. He hadn't thought her acceptance of the match would be quite so complete and so soon, and he was relieved. Had she continued her rebellion, he would have met it with all the strength at his command. Feeling smug with his triumph, he preceded her out the door and into the carriage. Now that he needn't worry about what Peterbroome could do to him, Grovenor intended to forget all about it and enjoy the evening ahead.

The ride to the Givens's party was an agony for Kate, eased only by the chance of meeting Charlie and Nick Monroe. Before her father had turned her life on end, she had made happy plans and schemes for introducing Nicholas Monroe to society, beginning with tonight's soiree. She had a short time to accomplish the task, and thinking about it now helped her keep her mind away from the twin and horrendous prospects of bethrothal and marriage to the last man on earth she wanted to share her life.

Kate quaked at the thought of what would happen after the month was up. Suicide or running away to lose herself in some dim, dark corner of England were possibilities she would have to consider, and very soon. But for tonight she wanted to help Charlie set matters in train for Nick, and she wanted no one to know the depths of her misery. If only she had someone to turn to.

Charlie had been saved from death and dishonor at the eleventh hour with the heaven-sent arrival of Nicholas Monroe into his life. Was there anyone to rescue her? She doubted it.

Her father's sulfurous rages and mistrust of everyone had long since alienated her mother's family and most of his own. The Grovenors were a small clan, a dying breed in fact. Her father and grandfather had been only children and, to her father's disgust, Kate's mother succeeded in producing only a daughter. His disappointment was the cause of many arguments between her parents. With the exception of cousin Lizbeth, who was poor as a churchmouse and cowered at Pearson Grovenor's approach, other family members kept to themselves and wanted nothing to do with father or daughter. It was strange that her father revered his ancestors but couldn't abide his few contemporaries.

As for turning for help to friends, that, too, was out of the question. In their circle no one dared interfere between father and daughter. With all the goodwill in the world, it simply wasn't done. Hot tears filled her eyes, and she hid them from him, having seen the triumph in her father as he looked at her before they left the house. Her tears would move him not at all. They had never done for her mother, and would be ineffective for her.

Kate often thought that women in her position, whatever their ages, were at the mercy of their fathers, and the more prominent the family, the fewer options for independence, unless they wanted to be thought of as freaks. Kate hated being a woman sometimes.

Chapter Eight

Nick circled the Givens's ballroom in Charlie's wake, acknowledging introductions to a dozen men and as many women, his eyes directed at the massively carved white and gold doorway, praying for a glimpse of Kate.

When at last she appeared, she was even more enchanting than he remembered, and he placed his hand on Slayton's sleeve.

Charlie turned and the penny dropped. The quivering of Nick's hand went through Slayton like an electric shock. Seeing Nick's face lit as if a thousand candles shone through, Charlie knew at once that Nick, too, had succumbed as so many others, himself included, to the spell she created around her. Charlie's sympathy went out to Nick, his own heart bruised and battered by a hopeless infatuation for Kate which, almost more than anything else, had made him the wastrel he was before Nick took him in hand.

It was a love on his part that started when they were both lonely and neglected children relegated to the country. Even if he had not become unworthy of Kate, her father would never have countenanced a match. Pearson hated Charlie's father, who was a second cousin, and his ambitions for Kate, his only child and heir, did not include throwing her away on a younger son.

All of this was going through Slayton's mind as he wove a path for himself and Nick through the crowd to Kate. One look was all Charlie needed to know that something of great moment had happened to Kate since he'd left her at her door early that afternoon. Charlie, with Nick at his heels, elbowed a dozen men who came up to her from all parts of the ballroom.

"Coz, how marvelous you look," Charlie said, taking her arm.

"Lady Katherine, are you well?" Like Charlie, Nick knew that Kate, for all her dazzling gown clung to her divine figure, was not the same radiant woman he'd spent the happiest hours of his life with dashing in and out of the shops that morning. Kate's eyes were blank, remnants of the tears she thought she'd brushed away in the carriage still hung on her lashes.

"You both clean up well," Kate hastened to say. And, indeed, they were the handsomest men in the room. The last thing she wanted was to spoil Nick's first London party with even a hint of her unhappiness. In time Charlie and Nick would know, as all London would, that she was promised to Peterbroome, and the waves of disbelief the news would certainly occasion were not to be thought of now.

Kate wove her arms through theirs and moved quickly into the room, pulling them along, knowing that they were becoming the center of attraction. Nick moved liked a Viking among most of the other men who attempted to surround them, and women stopped to ogle him as they passed. Kate was not a veteran of the London social wars for nothing. By morning this formidable stranger in their midst would be the next blue-eyed boy, the talk of the *ton*, and only the most heinous breach of conduct could stem a brilliant assault on the town. She still had a few doubts about society's biases against strangers, and she would watch and wait, and aid Nick in every way. It was a promise, and she kept her promises.

Kate experienced a sudden pride in herself and Charlie. They were doing something unselfish and worthwhile. As his sponsors, they had set him on his path to social acceptance, and she was certain Nick Monroe would be a great asset to society, which needed new blood and the new insights that he could give them.

"Now, Mr. Monroe, I hope you will find London kinder

than it has been heretofore," Kate said, adding, in an attempt at raillery, "Soon women will be at your feet and their men at your throat, if that is what you want."

"That is not at all what I want, dear Lady Katherine. I want only one woman."

Lucky woman, Kate said under her breath, leading them farther into the room.

"What have you planned for tomorrow in furtherance of Mr. Monroe's education, Charlie?" Kate inquired.

"I ask first that you call me Nick or Nicholas, but not Mr. Monroe," Nick asked softly. He desired more than anything to hear her say his name, so that in the succeeding months and years after he finally screwed up the courage to drop out of her life, he could add that to his memories of their short time together.

"Ah, lesson number one in the ways of London." Kate smiled. "A lady must be related or know a gentleman very well indeed before she uses his first name. Many married ladies I know never address their husbands by their given name, but I might stretch a point and call you 'Monroe,' if that will suit."

They agreed and proceeded amiably across the room until Peterbroome, drunk and staggering, came up to them and pulled Kate roughly away.

"I hear all is well with our betrothal," he said unsteadily. "Don't try to play games with me. We are going to marry."

"Take your hands off me. I am not your wife yet," Kate said coolly.

Peterbroome turned white and would have argued, but thought better of it. He stared daggers at Charlie and Nick, and reeled off.

"Oh, God, Kate, you can't be thinking of marrying Peterbroome, of all people?" Charlie asked, incredulous.

"The real question is what is my father thinking of?" she replied, visibly shaken. "I only found out this afternoon."

Nick took Kate's hand and settled it in the crook of his arm. He didn't understand all that had transpired, but if this golden girl was promised to the dark, menacing-looking man raging away, it would explain the change in her from the morning. Nick didn't need to know the man's history to dislike him on sight.

"I don't believe it," Charlie said, his shock at the news spilling over.

"That makes two of us," Kate said, shuddering.

"What are you going to do?"

Before Kate could reply, Peterbroome reappeared and separated her from Nick none too gently.

"This waltz is mine," he said, pulling Kate toward the other dancers, holding her close against him. "You are promised to me, and you are mine."

Kate was revolted. But any public display of distaste would alert everyone around them, and word would get back to her father. She could not chance that he would force her hand, when she needed all the time she could buy to think of some means to change his mind or arrange an escape.

"I have a month to make up my mind, and if you want my acquiescence, I suggest that you be patient," Kate said, her eyes daring him to push her further.

"Neither you nor your father have a choice in the matter," he said.

"What have you done to him?" Kate knew it was folly to ask, but she wanted to know, needed to know.

"Ask him." Peterbroome grinned wickedly, whirling her across the room, all attention riveted on them, making it impossible for her to press him with more questions.

When the waltz ended, Peterbroome returned her to Charlie and Nick, a possessive and leering smirk on his raddled face.

"She is yours—for the moment."

Boiling over with white-hot anger, Nick didn't need instructions on the niceties of London to know that with everyone at the ball watching them he couldn't attempt to take Peterbroome apart piece by piece. His hands clenched in fury. He wanted to smash the man's face, and promised himself that one day soon he would.

Beside him, Charlie was, for once in his life, at a loss for words, his distress pouring out of him like steam. He took

Kate's arm and left the ballroom, with Nick bringing up the rear.

"Kate, what is going on?"

"Don't plague me about Peterbroome, please. I still have a little while, and I mean to make the most of it," she said, trying for a lightness she was far from feeling. "I have made a list of things for Mr. Monroe to acquire, and I mean to see him get them."

Charlie knew his cousin well enough to know that any attempt to change her mind would be useless. Her mouth was grim, her eyes afire, sure signs that she could not be deterred from any course she was determined on.

"Lady Katherine, let me assure you that you needn't put yourself about for me, when you have other things on your mind," Nick interjected, overhearing the conversation. Her suffering was all too evident, and he didn't want to add to it. He saw no way to eliminate the cause, however much he tried.

"I have nothing more important to do than to resume shopping again tomorrow," Kate said with formidable determination, sweeping aside any argument. "You have to have accounts at Purdey's for guns and Berry Brothers for wines."

"Yes, Kate.," Charlie said.

"And, Charlie, we must go to Storr and Mortimer, the goldsmiths in Regent Street," Kate added wickedly. "I hear a colonel of the Guards gives them twenty-five pounds the quarter to keep him in new and different studs for his shirts every week during the season."

"Yes, I've heard the story," Charlie interposed. "The man's an ass."

"I prefer Tessier's on Bond Street for a quizzing glass, gold seals and chains, a silver snuff box, cigar case and cigar cutter," Kate said, warming to her subject.

She looked at them saucily and added, "Then, of course, there is Tattersall's for horses, carriages, dogs, and the like."

"Tattersall's?" Charlie laughed. "Surely you don't expect to accompany us there."

"Even if I am a better judge of horseflesh than you are?" Kate ragged him. It was a familiar argument from their shared childhood.

"Are you indeed?" Nick had meant to stand on the sidelines, but he was so pleased to see the ease with which Kate seemed to be throwing off the megrims caused by Peterbroome's untimely appearance. He was delighted to join in. "I rather fancy myself knowledgeable, but I can always learn more."

"That's settled then," Kate announced. "And now I desire nothing more than a glass of champagne."

Kate blessed Herr Hendricks for his training. She was still shaken to the core by the plot hatched between her father and Peterbroome, but from now on she was determined that no one would know of her misery. It was hard to remember that only a few days ago her major concern was the fear that people would learn that she had a second life as an actress. What irony. What a nonsense that had become in the light of her father's treachery. But she wouldn't think about that now. She turned a radiant face to Nick.

"Do you dance?"

"If you can call it that. Charlie tells me he is a famous teacher, and we have spent hours practicing, with his valet beating out the time and singing the tunes."

"He's quite good, actually," Slayton chimed in.

"Good. Champagne first, and then I shall find out for myself," Kate proposed.

Chapter Nine

A small, closed carriage drew up smartly before the giant doors of the Albany promptly at ten the next morning. A scowling Barkley held the reins.

"For Lord Charles Slayton, mate, and be quick about it," Barkley called out sullenly.

Nick and Charlie were just leaving the breakfast table when the summons came. They had been up half the night talking about Kate's marrying Peterbroome, and were still hashing it over.

"Peterbroome is the most outrageous man in London, a roué, and leader of the wildest set," Charlie was saying again. "But his lineage is impeccable. The trouble's his grandfather, who keeps him on short rations. That makes him dangerous at the card table and everywhere else."

Earlier Charlie had told Nick that Kate had turned down the most eligible men in town, a duke among them.

Nick could believe it. With every moment spent with her, he had become more enamored, while rating his chances of capturing her heart as less than impossible. If he couldn't have Kate for himself, he wanted her to be happy, but knew that she could never be with a bastard like Peterbroome. He knew his kind. He had met too many bad men in his travels not to recognize evil when he saw it. Peterbroome was that kind of man, a rotter through and through.

Nick was beside himself.

"Can't you do something, Charlie?" he pleaded.

"Not a thing. You don't know my uncle. He is the most stupid, stubborn man, who thinks he's very clever. He is proud as paint, thinking himself up to all the tricks on everything. He is, in fact, a joke among the *ton*, but still rich and powerful by virtue of name and fortune."

They quit the table and followed the Albany servant down the long, cavernous hall to the sunlit courtyard.

Barkley blanched at the sight of them. What was going on? First his mistress routs him out of bed in the middle of the night to send him on a wild errand and insists he play John Coachman in the bargain, and now this. What was the cove with Charlie Slayton about? He'd know him anywhere, the very man he'd shown the door to not that long ago. And here he was as cool as you please, poised to enter the carriage. All his protective instincts rose like bile, and he leaped to the ground bent on beating the Johnnie into the ground with his fists.

But Nick was too quick for him. His own shock at seeing Barkley, obviously a Grovenor servant, was no less shattering. He knew he had to do something. He shoved Charlie into the carriage first, saying he'd forgotten something.

He took Barkley aside, away from prying eyes. "I mean no harm to your lady. I swear it," Nick said. "She didn't recognize me, and I haven't said a word, and won't."

Barkley unclenched his fists. He didn't know why, but against all odds he believed the man.

"You hurt Lady Kate in any way, and I'll kill you," Barkley said, his threat backed by black certainty. "Word gets out she's an actress, she'll be ruined."

Nick nodded vigorously.

Eyeing Nick with lingering suspicion, Barkley returned to his perch.

Nick took a deep breath and entered the coach, and instead of Kate, he found a lithe young man, elegant legs crossed, smoking a slim cigar, sitting next to Charlie.

"Meet Mr. Smith, Nick." Charlie laughed. "She's taking us to Tattersall's, and God knows where else."

What a complete actress she was, Nick told himself. However it was accomplished, Kate made a truly bang-up blade, with a hint of down on her cheeks and makeup that had turned her from a stunning woman to a devastatingly handsome young sprig of the town.

"I don't believe it." Nick grinned. He was convinced that if he lived to be a hundred, he'd never see all the parts and talents that made Kate Grovenor the most fascinating woman he could ever hope to meet. And love. Each time they met, she showed him a new side he could admire.

Kate was delighted with the success of her little adventure. She took the gold-handled cane and tapped on the carriage roof, her head halfway out the window.

"Barkley, Hyde Park," she called out.

"My darling Kate, if I didn't know better, I'd say you were the most consummate actress in the world."

"I rather think I have possibilities." She giggled, enormously pleased her disguise was up to scratch. Faced with a sleepless night thinking about Peterbroome, Kate remembered she had played a Regency buck in one of Herr Hendricks's first productions for her. She sent Barkley to the theater to ransack the costume room. It had been an inspired thought, and she was able to fall asleep soon after Barkley returned. Trust ever faithful Barkley to save the day. And night.

"Now, Mr. Monroe, what would you be looking for in the way of cattle?"

"Several matched pairs, several hacks, and a hunter or two to be starting with, a traveling carriage for my mother, and a curricle and cabriolet for myself," Nick said, ticking off a list with decision.

"You don't believe in half-measures, do you?" Charlie asked.

"I mean to start the way I want to go on in my new life," Nick answered. "I've worked very hard to see my dreams come true for myself and my mother."

"Then you shall have them, and no place better to start than at old Tatt's," Kate interposed, warming toward Nick with every moment.

"Surely you will need some hounds for your place in Wiltshire," Slayton mentioned.

"I'd quite forgotten my needs for Delacourt House for the moment. The kennels are in sad repair. The previous owners let everything go to rack and ruin."

"Then you are the man who is buying the old pile. Papa mentioned that someone had bid for the place. I am so glad. It is a divine house. I have a school friend who lives close by."

"Then you must come and see it soon, Lady Kate," Nick said, with pride of ownership, until he recalled himself. What right had he to think of a future with Kate as part of it? Seeing her married to someone else would be a torment, but far worse knowing that the someone was evil incarnate, John Peterbroome.

"I shall hold you to your invitation," Kate said, settling back against the luxurious dove-gray squabs. "What pleasure it will be for you to set the place to rights." And what fun it would be to help him make it the showplace she knew he would. How wonderful to share such a house with someone so easy, such a free spirit, so open to every new experience. She was tired to death of the bleached-out, thrill-seeking dissolute men like Peterbroome, who had seen it all and done it all, overdressed, self-centered, blasé, drunken layabouts for all their great family trees.

An uncomfortable silence followed in the well-sprung carriage headed toward Hyde Park.

"Now, tell me what I should expect, so that I do not make a cake of myself by gaping," Nick asked, to relieve the sudden quiet that had descended on them.

"Well, let me tell you first what I have heard, and Charlie can fill in the rest," Kate said gaily. "It is a plaything for the pinks of the swells, the tulip of the goers, fox-hunting clericals, scions of nobility, roguish coachmen, saucy butchers, neat jockeys, et cetera, et cetera, et cetera—"

Kate ran out of breath and tried to go on, but Charlie interrupted.

"Forget what she said. Tattersall's is no ordinary place. It gives a tone to the sporting world in the same way that transactions on the 'Change give tone to the business world. 'Tis the only place where a nod from a stable keeper is as important to the auctioneer as a wink of a Right Honorable, if not more so."

"You're so lyrical this morning, Charlie," Kate said,

twitting him. "I wanted to give Mr. Monroe a picture of the atmosphere, you clunk."

In a few minutes Nick saw for himself all that they told him and more. Unlike the rough and dirty places in Australia and around the world where he went to buy horses, Tattersall's was elegant, clean, and stylish beyond his imagination. Thoroughbred horses, the like of which he had seldom seen anywhere in his travels, were paraded by immaculately liveried servants. The latest mode of carriages stood about, examined by practiced whipsters. It was everything he had been led to expect of London graciousness and innovation, and he didn't care if people knew him for what he was, a country oaf having the time of his life.

Kate found Nick's delight contagious, for, in truth, she had always wanted to see Tattersall's herself, and was just as impressed as he. Nick's childlike excitement touched her deeply, and she was rewarded when he took her arm and grinned like a boy with a new kite. He was so alive and racing to catch up with experiences he seemed to have missed in his life.

"You never fail to give me pleasure," he said feelingly, overcome when Kate's green eyes shone at him. He wasn't sure he hadn't gone too far, but he couldn't help himself. She was in every way his very own genie, who might one day disappear into her lamp, just when his love was hers forever.

Indeed, Nick's gratitude, simply expressed, was so movingly disingenuous and charmingly framed, it hit the mark. He was the kind of man who deserved all the cosseting she could give him. Yearned to give him, she amended, in astonishment.

She felt herself go pale and shivery. Oh, my God, Kate thought, suddenly breathless, as if someone or something was choking the life out of her. I love him! I love Nicholas Monroe, and I didn't know it until this very moment.

Kate turned abruptly, terrified she would give away her momentous discovery by look or gesture. She had known, but was afraid to admit even to herself that she was attracted to Nick as to no other man in her life, so quickly, so unexpectedly. What a fool she was not to know until now what she was capable of feeling for a man! Sweet love. Giving love.

Kate didn't know where to turn, what to do, so stunning was the realization that she was like every woman, capable of falling deeply, headlong, irretrievably in love.

So this is what she had seen in Barbara Maitland and Colby Browning, when their eyes lit like beacons, talking of their husbands. No one needed to tell Kate that her heart had never been stirred, and that was the reason she had long been heir to the terrible possibility that she was cold toward men and likely to remain so. With the way she felt for Nick Monroe no longer in doubt, Kate knew for certain that marriage to John Peterbroome would be worse than intolerable. She was well and truly trapped.

The Fates that had at long last given her a glimpse of heaven, were snatching it away all too quickly.

Near tears, Kate went in search of Charlie in Tattersall's famous taproom. She must distance herself from Nick at once, or she'd do something outrageous and disgrace herself. And then where would she be? *A nice man pays me a graceful compliment, and I dissolve in tears.*

Charlie watched in horror when men swiveled at Kate's appearance in the doorway of the noisy room. He moved quickly. Too many men whom he knew in the place had predilections for handsome young striplings. They smiled too quickly at Kate in eager anticipation of conquests. Against all Charlie's and Nick's very sound fears of detection, they had managed to carry off Kate and her disguise in fine style by keeping her from Tattersall's regulars. They'd been lucky so far, but he wasn't going to chance a misadventure at this juncture. It could be a major disaster for Kate's reputation, and that was the last thing he wanted. Her dragon of a father would have his ears. He was not a fearful man at most times, but Charlie had no wish to encounter Peterbroome's wrath either.

Charlie took Kate's arm and led her back to a corner in the stable yard. He saw the tears hovering in her eyes.

"What happened?"

"Oh, Charlie, I am so unhappy." Kate hadn't meant to reveal her heart, and was appalled that she could lose her way so easily.

"I can't tell you, but, oh, how I would love to tell someone," Kate whispered to her cousin.

"Is it Peterbroome? I may often seem a sad rattle, but I do love you, Kate," Charlie said. "Tell me. Maybe I can help."

"Of course it's Peterbroome, but even worse than that," Kate said with a sardonic laugh. "But don't worry. I shall deal with it. I must."

Nick came around a corner. He slowed his steps. Everything about Kate, her slim shoulders now cast down, the way she kneaded her hands, was so unlike the girl she was before he had misspoken. Had he given himself away? It had to be. He must watch himself in the little time before her betrothal was formally announced. Nothing would make him press their friendship once that happened. He couldn't bear seeing her in Peterbroome's arms or imagining him in Kate's bed. The very idea of them together almost sent him over the edge. He continued to walk toward them, determined to keep himself in check.

"Good man. Kate's got the headache and is going home," Charlie called out as Nick came up to them. It was a lame excuse, but he couldn't think of anything that would prevent a long discussion that would agitate Kate even more.

Nick nodded, and the trio walked silently toward the entrance where the Grovenor carriage had been hidden from curious eyes. Nick handed Kate in and signaled Barkley to leave.

"It was more than a headache, wasn't it?" Nick asked, heading back to Tattersall's with Charlie. "Was it something I said?"

Charlie caught on at once. He recalled Kate saying she was upset about Peterbroome, and worse. He needed to know what worse meant.

"I think we need to go to my club for a drink," Slayton

said, making for St. James's Street. A block away, he turned to Nick.

"Is Kate your Lady in Gray?"

Startled, Nick nodded. Trust Charlie to remember how he had referred to Kate in one of their first all-night conversations soon after they returned to London. He thanked his stars, he had omitted all the circumstances of his first meeting with Kate. With everything else to plague her, he would have been devastated to have revealed Kate's furtive career to her cousin. His foresight was cold comfort to him.

"Does Kate suspect you knew her before I introduced you?"

"I have done my best to be circumspect, but I may have been a little unwise today, a little too ardent," Nick replied morosely. He told Charlie what he had said that seemed to upset Kate at Tattersall's.

"Nothing in that," Charlie said dismissively. On the other hand, Slayton's quick wit told him he and Nick might both be wide of the mark. Could it be that Kate was succumbing to Nick? Why not? Hadn't he warmed to Nick within moments after the blotched holdup? Hadn't he seen women at the ball last night lose their poise over Nick's wide shoulders and Greek-god profile? Why should Kate, as womanly as any of them, resist such physical perfection?

Charlie knew in his bones that he had hit on the only logical reason for Kate's losing her composure so suddenly. Poor Kate. If her father was venal enough to marry her off to the cold-blooded Peterbroome and something happened to the betrothal, old Pearson would look even higher and never settle for a son-in-law fresh from the wilds of Australia. Like all Englishmen, he believed that faraway place was only suitable for the criminal classes.

By the time he and Nick were nearing the Palladian splendor of Brooks, he had worked out the equation to his satisfaction, if not his approval. He needed time to think about his next move, and walked casually toward the three-story, Corinthian-columned building that dominated the street.

Nick stopped in his tracks, overcome by the grandeur.

The first-floor balcony running the length of the club made it look like many of the private country residences he'd seen on his way to Delacourt House. He loved the classic lines, the strength and power it represented, but hated the way it made him feel, insignificant and loutish. What the hell am I playing at? What am I doing here anyway? For twopence I'd turn around and run for my life.

"Am I dressed properly for your grand friends?" He was furious with himself. Never one to make much of his appearance until he met Charlie and decided to do everything sartorially correct, he had become self-conscious about the way he looked. If he didn't watch himself, he'd become a male milliner. Even so, he didn't want to disgrace Charlie in, of all places, his famous club. Never for a moment did Nick forget what his friend was doing for him. It was a rare honor that Charlie was conferring on a man he knew for such a short time. Nick had no desire to become a member of Brooks, but he couldn't deny how much he wanted to see what this and all the other clubs were like. He was curious about the life and practices of London's blue bloods, even if he had no desire to be one himself.

"You'll make the chaps envious," Charlie said, glad of the few minutes more he had to decide what he would say to Nick. He surveyed the superb blue superfine coat with gold buttons and the slim, gray trews. Abe Ellis and his workmen had spent the night running them up for Nick and had delivered them to the Albany before they woke that morning. Charlie pronounced them perfect.

A good haircut was in order, but that could wait for later in the day. The important thing was the clothes he and Kate had chosen the day before had turned Nick into a model of fashion. Beau Brummell would have approved this first step in the transformation of the big Australian into a proper London dandy. Charlie could not have been more pleased. Nick Monroe was a companion to make anyone proud. He felt a little like Pygmalion.

Charlie clapped Nick on the back, and they entered the imposing corner building at St. James's and Park streets. With Nick looming next to him, Charlie exchanged greetings and introductions with all manner of men in the two-story entry dominated by a pastel painting of Charles James Fox.

"Fox was the great Whig statesman and orator," Charlie explained.

"Yes. I've heard of him, of course," Nick replied through frozen lips.

Nick was an immediate success. Charlie basked in the warmth of the greetings from the cream of London male elite. They looked Nick up, down, and sideways, in a well-bred but covert way, of course, and seemed to approve. A few held back, but most obviously liked what they saw. Charlie was especially proud when staid men, who had ignored him in the last few years of his disgraceful existence, came forward to greet them.

Charlie knew from the beginning that Nick's formidable figure and natural dignity would give him greater preference over most men seeking entrance into the inner precincts represented by Brooks's membership. But seeing the exceptional interest startled even Charlie. In the ordinary course, London elite might not like a stranger in their midst, but then not many strangers looked or comported themselves like Nicholas Monroe. Charlie could see their interest and curiosity were aroused. He had counted on that. The first major hurdle in Nick's climb to acceptance had been easily scaled, and Kate would be well pleased when he gave her an account of it. He looked forward to telling her at the theater that night.

For Nick it was a mesmerizing experience. Never in his most roseate dreams as a dirty-faced, tattered little urchin intent on making something of his future had he dared see himself striding the hallowed halls of one of England's most celebrated institutions. He had never been so lofty in his ambitions. Vivian Monroe had inspired her son's dreams, but even she had never aimed so high for him.

All this was going through Nick's mind while following Charlie through one room after another. He wasn't sure what Charlie was looking for, until they settled in the library, another of the magnificently proportioned rooms.

This one was filled with sturdy old bookshelves, fine tables haphazardly strewn among leather chairs and sofas, the whole dominated by portraits, ancient silver, and ornaments. Charlie ordered tea for himself and a brandy for Nick from a club servant, and led him to an especially secluded corner near massive windows.

While they waited, Charlie gossiped and smoked. He was not at ease, but he didn't want Nick to know it. The moment he dreaded had arrived, and he was unable to think of an opening gambit that would not hurt Nick too much. Things had to be said, and it could be fatal to the happiness of Nick and Kate if he didn't proceed cautiously and firmly.

"Did I acquit myself to your satisfaction?" Nick asked, uncomfortably aware of Charlie's unusually somber mood. "Did I do something terrible?"

"You were admirable, old boy, admirable," Charlie replied absently as the servant hovered over them.

"Don't fence with me, Slayton," Nick said impatiently. "Something is bothering you."

"I need to know, are you in love with Kate?" he asked.

"Yes, damn your eyes. Is it so obvious?"

Charlie nodded, vigorously wishing he had never pledged to forgo strong drink. He needed Dutch courage, and tea gave him little of that.

"I am sorry, Nick, but I had to ask. And I have to say Kate can never marry you."

"Don't you think I know?" Nick found little solace in the assurance that he had been right about his chances of winning Kate from the moment her carriage left the stage door of the seedy theater. "Kate doesn't think of me as anything more than a momentary diversion. And I expected nothing more."

Slayton wanted to tell Nick that his love was returned in equal part, but caution made him hold his tongue. If he was right and Kate had formed a tendre for Nick, it might give Nick hope, and that would be disastrous.

"I'd make a far better husband than Peterbroome, but what's that to say to anything?" Nick said, crushing his cigar in a tray between his long, strong fingers, wanting it to be arrogant, dissipated Peterbroome's neck. "Her father must be a devil to wish her a life with that brute."

"Grovenor is a misanthropic bastard. I might as well confess a secret I tried to drown in drink." Charlie couldn't bear the bleak look on his friend's face. "If it helps, I am his victim, too. I have been hopelessly in love with Kate for years. I broached the subject to him in this very room one night after I came down from Oxford, and he made mincemeat of me in front of his friends. He detests my father and, by extension, hates me."

"Does Kate know how you feel?"

"She hasn't a clue, and never will. I trust you will not violate my confidence."

"What do you take me for?" Nick wasn't surprised by the confession. In the few short weeks since the aborted holdup, Nick was convinced that Charlie's wastrel ways hid deep secret pain. And if he, too, felt the despair of loving Kate in silence, then drink and gambling could be too easy, if useless, antidotes.

"What a fine tangle we are in," Charlie said desolately. "Kate is mistaking matters if she thinks that a few weeks will change her father's or Peterbroome's resolve. She suspects there may be something havey-cavey about all this, but I can assure you marriage to Peterbroome is a fait accompli."

Charlie's sentiments were his as well, but Nick couldn't bear the idea of standing by without making a push to help Kate.

"You told me that Captain Maitland has extraordinary resources," Nick said, his thoughts whirling like mad.

"Yes. Tarn has this fabulous group of men, called by many Londoners 'Maitland Marines.' They know where the bodies are buried in the life of everybody who is anybody," Charlie said, at a loss to know where Nick's mind was heading.

"Let us test them."

"What are you about?"

"If Kate were to be resigned to this marriage, I would be

miserable, but I could leave the field to Peterbroome and try to forget I ever met her," Nick said bitterly. "But you and Kate have given me to understand that there is something odd about the whole affair."

"That's wishful thinking, and you know it, Nick," Charlie argued. "My great-uncle knows Peterbroome's reputation as well as I do. All he cares about is attaching himself to Peterbroome's illustrious grandfather and his family. He's a ranking snob who doesn't care two pins for Kate's feelings, and never has."

"I am afraid you're right, but I will never be content until I know the truth of it."

Charlie could see that Nick was grasping at straws, and remained silent. If it gave him comfort to think he could scotch the hateful marriage, he, for one, wasn't about to disabuse Nick further. He thought he knew enough about Monroe, despite the recent vintage of their friendship, to suspect that the Australian was tenacious to a fault.

"What do you think Tarn Maitland can do that we can't do?" Charlie asked.

"That is what I mean to find out," Nick replied, downing the last drop of his drink and rising to his feet.

Chapter Ten

Kate's eyes, heavy and gritty from lack of sleep and weeping, roamed the boxes at Drury Lane that night hoping for a glimpse of Nick Monroe before the curtain went up on a performance of Edmund Kean in *The Merchant of Venice*.

At any other time, the chance to see the great Shakespearean actor in his most celebrated role was an occasion of great expectation for her. Kean was the acknowledged master performer of the age, and she often studied his acting and seductive voice for clues to employ in her own performances. But tonight the actor and the play were not the thing, but an excuse to test her newfound and disturbing knowledge that she had at long last found love.

When moments later the play began and the others in her father's box stopped chattering like demented crows, Kate spied Nick and Charlie across the theater. Her heart gave a titanic tilt, and she returned their greetings with the first happiness she felt since her world came crashing down. If Kate had any doubts about her feelings for Nick, they were dispelled like a heavy cloud. Nick was the handsomest and most vivid man in the audience, and she was not the only one who was aware of him. The other women in her party gasped and whispered among themselves.

Dressed in severe, elegant black evening attire, Nick stood head and shoulders above the mincing, colorful Bond Street fops, uniformed and bemedaled officers, and the women weighted down in jewels and satins.

"So that is the great mystery man Charlie Slayton has in tow," said the Countess of Aver, her father's latest rapacious paramour. "Aver met him at Brooks this afternoon, and said he was the talk of the club. I must get Slayton to introduce me."

Kate and her father turned to the aging beauty sitting between them. Her father, a coxcomb of the worst sort, was infuriated and fairly sizzled in anger. Kate was about to say something cutting, but bit back the words. Hadn't she prophesied Nick's effect on the jaded ladies of the *ton*? Hadn't she herself tumbled into love so quickly it fair made her head spin? In the name of heaven, was she at long last feeling jealous? The very idea was so foreign to her that she blushed at the thought of it.

If she had been feeling oppressed at the thought of being wed to Peterbroome, it was nothing to how she felt after she left Nick and her cousin at Tattersall's. Reality had struck later as she lay across her bed in a wave of agony about the future and the first intimations of the pain of wanting a man she could never have.

The interval came at last, and Kate begged to be allowed to remain. When her father rose to shepherd his guests from the box, Charlie and Nick came upon them. Kate could see her father was on the point of giving them the cut direct, but the ladies begged to be introduced. Enjoying the drama, Charlie insisted on presenting Nick, and the women were in seventh heaven, making a fuss that irritated Grovenor to near apoplexy.

Pearson Grovenor finally had his way and led the party out of the box. Kate tried to still her nerves. It would be hell on earth if she gave way to all she felt.

"Charlie, you never said you were taking Mr. Monroe to Brooks," Kate said, tapping her fan against his velvet sleeve.

"And have you force your way in on my coattails? Not a hope, my dear coz."

"Tell me what it was like, Mr. Monroe. I have wanted to see a man's club all my life."

"It was quite astounding. So imposing, so grand," Nick said, pretending not to notice that Kate was looking frail and worn down. He wanted to take her in his arms and kiss away the tried lines around her eyes and return them to their emerald brilliance.

"Did you see the card room?" Kate asked, giving a performance of nonchalance worthy of her teacher's impossible standards, when, in fact, all she longed to do was feast her eyes on Nick. But she pushed herself to chatter inconsequentially, hoping she made sense.

"Papa claims to have been at both Brooks and White's when Charles Fox astounded the *ton* with his feats of gambling, drinking, and political faithfulness all at once."

Charlie was immediately interested. "What story is that?"

Kate was vastly relieved to tell of how Fox once played faro at Brooks for twenty-two consecutive hours, from seven A.M. on a Tuesday until five A.M. on the Wednesday, and lost a shocking 1,000 guineas.

"On Thursday, he addressed the House of Commons, sat up drinking at White's until seven A.M., Friday. Then he crossed the road to Brooks and won 6,000 pounds. He left thereafter for Newmarket to bet on the races that same afternoon," Kate concluded with awe.

"I don't know another young woman in all London who would care, much less sparkle at the retelling of such a masculine accomplishment as you do," Charlie chided.

"I own many women lose fortunes over the card table, but the rest of us lead lives of supreme boredom that such a story, speaking for myself, is quite delightful to hear. I wish I'd been a fly on the wall and had seen it all. You know you would, too, Charlie Slayton."

"You have such an utterly romantic nature," her cousin said and laughed.

Charlie had been standing to the side of the box hoping to observe his two favorite people for signs of mutual attraction, and his study told him all and more than he needed to know. Kate's chatter might fool Nick, but not him. He hadn't a doubt that Kate returned Nick's regard in full measure. It hurt a great deal when he had never been able to raise more than cousinly affection. Yet Nick, without even trying, had claimed her within a few days. How terrible. All this love would do neither of them a pot of good.

Like most women he knew, Kate would never defy her father in any important matter. She was a woman of her time and as hidebound in tradition as any simpering country squire's daughter who wouldn't dream of marrying any man except the one her father approved for her.

It was a painful lesson he would have to teach Nick over and over again, no matter how much he and Kate hated Peterbroome.

An awkward pause descended on them, and Charlie quickly said the first thing that came into his mind.

"You would have been proud of our protégé. Nick bowled them out at the club," Charlie boasted. "Everyone wants to meet him. We were quite wide of the mark about the prejudices of our friends."

"They accepted me generously because Charlie told them I was the cause of his return to society and sobriety," Nick protested.

Kate could not doubt it. Charlie was fast returning to the lithe, devilishly blithe spirit she remembered when he was first sent down from Oxford and when they were children together. And all because Nick Monroe had given him a second chance at life and, she suspected, by some strange alchemy, had given Charlie some of his own strength and direction.

Could lightning strike twice in one family? Could the gods smile upon her and make this remarkable man love and change her life, too? Kate knew the answer was no. Men like Nick Monroe loved once and for all time. If indeed, as Charlie had told her from the beginning, Nick had given his heart away soon after he came to London, no other woman could win him. Certainly, least of all one like herself who didn't know the first thing about the arts and artifices of attaching a man's interest.

If, as I have been told, I left a trail of broken hearts in my wake, it was not due to anything I ever did, Kate reminded herself.

As the interval drew to a close, Nick called to her and

forced Kate out of her reverie. She promised to have supper with them at Lord Winterwood's house following the play just before her father and his friends returned to the box, bringing with them the last man on earth she wanted to see. Kate paled at the sight of Peterbroome ordering Nick and Charlie aside to bow low over her hand, his oily addresses taking away all the animation that seeing Nick had brought to her. The tension in the box was palpable, and she pleaded silently with Nick and Charlie to leave.

Chapter Eleven

Nick ascended the winged stairs of Lord Winterwood's Belgravia mansion behind Charlie Slayton, still smarting from his latest black encounter with Peterbroome. He scowled at the hordes of guests who brushed past him in haste to be seen by their host before attacking the groaning supper tables.

For twopence he would chuck the whole thing; but he knew he wouldn't. Kate had promised to meet them, and Charlie assured him that he would at last see the legendary Captain Maitland and Lord Browning.

As good as his promise, Charlie made short work of people who would delay their progress, slowing his pace only when they approached a large, open reception room well out of reach of the orchestra. Nick didn't need anyone to tell him who, of the half-dozen couples occupying the room, were the paragons he was to meet at last. It was more than just the warmth of their greeting for Charlie, but the way in which the men and their wives included him, a perfect stranger.

The women, one fair-haired and the other dark, would have claimed his admiration anywhere, even if Charlie hadn't whispered that they were the best examples of aristocratic Englishwomen. They were smiling, exceedingly attractive, modishly dressed, but not at all flamboyant, unlike many women he met since Kate and Slayton had launched him into society. Nick could see for himself that Barbara Maitland and Colby Browning—it was immaterial which was which—were fitting consorts for their husbands. While envy was not one of Nick's besetting sins, he couldn't help sensing perfect love and harmony between the husbands and wives, a state of affairs he wanted for himself. Quite suddenly marriage seemed a lovely thought, if the bride was Kate, of course.

The men, both tall and of astonishing good looks, rose to meet Nick, their hands outstretched in welcome. Charlie performed the introductions, and Nick quickly put the names with the faces. The fragile blonde was Lady Barbara; and the other, more strongly built, was Lady Colby.

"The black-haired swashbuckler is Captain Maitland, and the Viking devil is Lord Nevil Browning," Charlie explained.

Nick was enchanted with the way he was received. He met more people than he could ever hope to remember in the short time since Charlie and Kate had befriended him, but few who had seemed so genuinely pleased to accept him so warmly into their world.

Charlie charmingly explained who Nick was and how they'd met, heavily editing and passing over the holdup.

"I think Australia is one of the most breathtakingly beautiful places I have ever been," Maitland said pleasantly. "Were you born there?"

"No. It's a very long story, sir," Nick replied uncomfortably, almost writhing under Maitland's piercing dark eyes. He had a lot to tell Maitland about Australia, but he wasn't about to vent his spleen before the gently reared ladies. What he had told Kate was only the tip of the iceberg of English wrongs in the whole matter of transportation. He didn't want to offend their innocence or lose whatever good opinion they might have of him at this early stage. Nick shifted from one foot to the other, trying to think of something innocuous to say.

At once Lady Barbara sized up Nick's discomfort. She couldn't read its meaning or origins, but she knew when men were introduced to her husband for help and didn't want a woman about. Tarn's famous open purse and tender conscience were among the reasons she had fallen in love with the strikingly handsome mariner. Hadn't his kind heart overlooked her poverty and crippled leg when even her own brother had consigned her to the dustheap?

Barbara's eyes twinkled, and she pushed back her chair.

"I say, Colby, there is Kate Grovenor coming this way," Barbara said, taking her walking stick from where it rested next to the table. "We must discuss some charity matters with her."

The men rose.

"And now, Mr. Monroe," Maitland said, returning to his chair.

"I congratulate you, sir. Your fair lady is very perceptive," Nick said admiringly. Now that he had Tarn's attention, he didn't know where to start.

"Lady Barbara has had a great deal of experience with men who want to be private with her husband," Nevil Browning offered, his voice bland but his eyes wary of the stranger at their table.

"You mean people always want something from the captain?" Nick said, not at all sure at the moment that he wanted to be one of that legion.

"I suspect, Mr. Monroe, you are not a man who asks favors easily," Maitland observed openly, weighing the Australian sitting across from him. Tarn prided himself on his ability to read people. Without boasting, he considered it the single most important talent he had, and the reason for his success. He really believed it was a gift, and never took it for granted. After all, the reason for his marvelous wife, wondrously happy marriage, and four beautiful children was his unerring judgment of people. The first time he saw Lady Barbara Worth, he knew she was extraordinary, despite her frail appearance and disastrous life. Other men had dismissed her as a poor nonentity from an impoverished, worthless family.

"I wouldn't be where I am without the leg up I received from time to time." Tarn concluded his survey of his rich inner history while judging the man next to him.

Nick nodded, not at all disconcerted by Maitland's frank appraisal. He hoped he passed muster with the big, quiet man dressed, as his cognomen described so aptly, in dazzling white linen and a fine black evening suit. At once he understood why Kate and Charlie sang Captain Black and White's praises. His was an overwhelming personality, and even if Nick didn't know how powerful and highly regarded Maitland was, one look at the man would have told him he'd met a paragon. There were few men who daunted Nick Monroe, but Maitland succeeded in tying him and his tongue in knots without trying.

"Now, how can I be of service to you, Mr. Monroe?" Tarn asked in his rumbling baritone.

All at once Nick was at a loss where to begin and how much to say. He appealed to Charlie.

"Nick wants your help, Captain, in addressing the cruelty shown to people transported to Australia," Charlie said, coming to his rescue as if on cue.

"How odd you are concerned about the plight of convicts, when you look as if you have prospered in Australia, perhaps even at the terrible expense of the cheap convict labor one hears about," Nevil Browning said, openly sneering. "Have you a bad conscience?"

Bridling, Nick leaped to his feet prepared to quit the room, the fashionably noisy party, the false life his susceptible heart and loins catapulted him into.

"You are dead wrong on all counts, my lord." His eyes narrowed to slits. *How could I have been so wrong to trust these men? By God, my judgment is becoming warped by my love for Kate and my pathetic desire to be a part of a world I don't belong in. Well, I have come to my senses, and the scales are off my eyes. To men like Browning and Maitland, I will always be a yahoo.*

Nick turned and began to quit the room.

"Browning wanted to see what you were made of. We both did," Tarn said, moving with swift panther grace to stop Nick and bring him back to the table.

"I apologize profoundly, Mr. Monroe," Nevil Browning added shamefacedly. "I am naturally suspicious of men who make fortunes on the backs of unfortunates. Some get religion or philanthropy, or both. Their consciences, their

dreams of a title or success in society often make them
wish to wipe clean the past."

Nick stared blankly at the man, recalling the years he and
his mother subsisted on scraps and slops, either cold as ice
or hot as hell, dressed like beggars, outcasts, with no one to
turn to for help until he was old enough to fight their way
out of abject privation by his fists and his wits.

"I am unashamedly the son of a convict." Each word
came out etched in acid. Nick studied the faces of the three
men turned toward him. "My father was a solicitor's clerk
tricked into taking the punishment for a crooked peer's precious son," Nick said, his voice bleak.

"My father lived in hell and was subject to terrible degra-
dations slaving for a depraved farmer who starved him and
later beat him to death," Nick said, fighting down the hor-
rific memories. "Those are my credentials, sir, in asking
your help for the poor souls your government sends to Australia for the least and the worst of crimes. Some, like my
father, were innocent, but no one would listen."

Not even Browning's goading would make Nick talk
about the deprivations he and his mother endured during
their early days in Australia. He had learned that nightmares did not always disappear in the light of day, nor were
they necessarily lightened by revealing the truth.

Browning cleared his throat.

"My wife tells me my tongue runs ahead of my head,"
said Browning, flushing furiously. Sheepishly he extended
his hand. "I had no right to question your motives. How can
we be of service?"

Nick swallowed hard, debating whether to take Lord
Browning's hand.

"Actually, Nick has need of your service on two fronts,
but this is not the time or place," Charlie interposed
quickly. The women were crossing the room toward them,
led by an exercised Kate Grovenor, and he didn't want
them to hear anything that would reduce Nick in their eyes.

Beyond that, Slayton was distressed for Nick. He had
suspected he suffered some indignities in his life, but the

last thing he expected to hear was that his father had been judged a criminal.

If ever Charlie's reckless and romantic heart secretly hoped to unite his cousin and his savior, the awful truth of Nick's origins made it unthinkable. Even if he could prove his father's innocence, no aristocratic father, even one far kinder than Pearson Grovenor, would ever bless such a union.

"Have you agreed to help Mr. Monroe?" Kate asked, coming up to them, willing Tarn and Nevil to give Nick whatever he wanted.

"We will use our good offices, but it won't be easy," Tarn told her. "Governments move very slowly, especially when they can rid themselves of people they deem nuisances, make a profit which is actually a loss, and settle a country they've conquered but don't know what to do with afterward."

"All governments like to hide their venality in clean cloth, Kate," Nevil agreed.

"And now I see that my dear Barbara is showing signs of fatigue, and in her condition I think it wise we leave at once."

The party broke up. But too soon for Nick. In Maitland, he sensed the only solution for Kate's terrible straits. If Maitland was just being kind and would try to help him achieve his goals, that was one thing, but what about Kate and the despicable Peterbroome? How long would Peterbroome and Kate's father be patient? The month's grace was too short. Moreover, he'd heard and seen enough to be certain that neither man could be trusted to consider the tender feelings of a woman.

Smiling his apologies to Lady Barbara, Nick presumed on her generosity once again. "One more kindness, my lady."

She nodded and moved off to join the others.

"I know it's not the done thing to betray a confidence, but do bear with me, sir," he whispered. "Slayton and I have learned that Lady Katherine's father has sanctioned her betrothal to Lord Peterbroome. She is desperate to find a way out."

At first annoyed about the intrusion, Maitland stopped in his tracks.

"I don't believe it."

"It's true, sir. Can you help us?"

Nick wanted to cut off his tongue. He'd betrayed Kate and his own feelings in one move.

"So that's it. Have you, like so many others, fallen in love with the Charmer?"

"I want only her happiness."

"Of course," Maitland said, smiling before the hopelessness of the younger man's cause. "You are asking for the moon, Monroe."

"I know there's no chance for me, and she doesn't even know I exist in that way," Nick said. "She hates Peterbroome, and I am afraid she will do something terrible if he's forced on her."

"I can't help Kate," Maitland said sorrowfully. "I am a father myself, and hope for a daughter one day soon. I would never come between a man and his daughter. Never."

"Would you have Peterbroome for your daughter?"

"You devil," Maitland said, tight-lipped.

"There's something suspicious about the betrothal, I am certain, sir."

"That's wishful thinking, and you know it." Maitland left to go to his wife, then stopped. "On the face of it, the marriage is eminently suitable. They come from renowned and respected families."

Maitland walked a few steps, turned around again, and looked Nick straight in the eye, whispering, "I can't stop the marriage, but I can gain you some time."

He called out, "Kate, help this young man write a brief stating all his arguments for the sorry state of affairs in Australia. There have been others presented and rejected. One more can't hurt."

Maitland peered over his shoulder and winked at Nick.

Chapter Twelve

In perfect charity with the world, Nick had forgotten all his resolve of the night before to forgo the pleasures of society and allow Kate to drift out of his life.

That was yesterday, before Tarn Maitland gave him the gift of time with his Kate.

Kate received Nick in the morning room, her maid sitting quietly in a corner. Quills sharpened to dagger points and stacks of the best vellum purchased that morning at Starr's in Bond Street covered a delicate Queen Anne table.

Shyness overcame them, and they welcomed the interruption of the family butler and a handsome footman carrying a massive silver tray with a light lunch. With the departure of the menservants, another uncomfortable silence threatened.

Kate searched her mind for something to say that would bridge their awkwardness and put them back on their old footing.

"I have often wondered if newly married people worry about what they will find to talk about after the ceremony," she said airily.

Halfway through, Kate realized she was making a terrible faux pas. The man will think I have designs on him. That tears it. I have really made a fool of myself this time, talking of marriage. How could I have said anything so stupid? Oh, why didn't Herr Hendricks teach me how to act in such a situation? Although what Shakespeare could do for her now escaped her for the moment. Kate thought longingly of her life before Nick and Peterbroome, when she spoke her mind and could be herself.

I didn't know how well off I was when my only concern was my next role, or what I would wear to what party. Now I am head-over-heels in love with a man who loves some-one else and doesn't even know I exist, except as a teacher of English etiquette! Kate steered her mind off the real blight in her life, marriage to John Peterbroome, and a shudder overtook her.

"Is something troubling you, Lady Kate?"

Nick quickly came to her side and took her hand. It was dry and hot when he brought it to his lips.

He was being kind and Kate knew she should take her hand away, but she couldn't, wanting more than anything to feel his lips on hers, wanting more than anything to rest her lips against the gleaming dark hair. She lifted her hand to touch Nick's hair.

"What the hell is going on here?" her father stood at the door, his deeply creased forehead and bulbous nose a map of dissipation, eyes glowering red like fire.

Kate quickly stepped between Nick and her father and in the most calculating and conciliatory voice attempted to smooth the waters.

"You know Mr. Monroe," she said easily. "I think you will be pleased, Papa. Your good friend, Captain Maitland, sent Mr. Monroe to seek my help in the preparation of a document for the Foreign Secretary."

Kate's desperation to avoid a scene gave genius to her wit. "Mr. Monroe knows few people, and you know I would do anything for Captain Black and White."

Clearly the name Maitland was a magic balm to this dis-solute fop dressed inappropriately like some slim-hipped, obnoxiously preening young London buck.

"Well, if Tarn Maitland vouches for you, young man, I shall say no more," Grovenor said grudgingly and departed.

"That was an inspired thought, mentioning Maitland." Nick laughed in mock despair, falling back against the pil-lows of a small sofa. "I thought I was going to be horse-whipped or challenged to a duel."

"My father has a genius for collecting important people and bragging about them, especially if they can't abide him." She was at once contrite. "What you must think of me, talking about my father this way," she groaned, wanting to hide her head in her hands. "Please forgive me. I am not always so cruel or unfilial."

Nick went to Kate and placed a hand on her shoulder. "I hope you feel you can say these things to me because you trust me and know me to be your friend."

And what if that isn't enough for me anymore? Kate wanted to shout. But years of breeding and a guarded heart prevailed. She had almost given herself away before her father interrupted them. It would never happen again. All Nick Monroe wanted of her was friendship, when she wanted, more than anything else in the world, to be all in all to him. Mistress? Yes. Wife? Oh, yes. Anything, but not his friend. Never that. It was all flesh and blood could bear to be near him and not want to be in his arms, in his bed, in his life forever, anything but a friend.

How quickly my fear of having a man touch me, hold me, disappeared once a tall, broad-shouldered Australian came into my life and, in all innocence, turned me into a panting, quivering animal practically begging for his caresses. She was ashamed, lost to decency.

What a travesty to have been the object of the desire of a hundred men and not to have had a scintilla of sense about what love meant. She knew about it now, and it was a hard lesson that made her sleepless with longing to have Nick with her, to have him need her as much as she needed him. Almost from the first time she saw him her dreams grew ever more disturbing and unsatisfied, with sensations in the very core of her womanhood she didn't understand or know how to gratify.

"Kate, are you ill?" Nick was standing before her at a loss, baffled by her silence.

She laughed. "I think we would be wise to begin working on your case," Kate said, rousing herself with effort and going to the table. "Where shall we start?"

Chapter Thirteen

Nick Monroe's smart, new, high-perched phaeton delivered that day by Tattersall's, wheeled away from the Manchester Square home of the Maitlands, with Kate, Nick, and Charlie feeling larky after a sumptuous tea.

"Whatever did you two find to say about Australia that could take both sides of ninety pages?" Charlie said in mock horror. "I don't envy Maitland the task of reading all your sensational charges."

Beside him, Kate bristled and turned on him like a tigress, so unlike the Kate of old.

"Mr. Monroe didn't make wild accusations," Kate said, leaping to Nick's defense. "He cited chapter and verse for the most heinous cases of cruelty and injustice I've ever heard."

Nick chuckled at her vehemence, but Charlie seeing more than anger, fell into a trouble silence. Kate was clearly overwhelmed by Nick and saw everything from a skewed vantage point. He'd been against Kate's role in helping Nick from the beginning. Put a beautiful woman in a room with a devastatingly virile man like Nick Monroe and anything can happen. He had voiced his objections, carefully couched to be sure, to both of them over the week the project took to complete.

"I know what you're trying to say, Charlie, but I assure you I was a perfect gentleman," Nick had answered him severely one evening in the coffee room at White's. "I may not have had all your advantages, but my mother is an educated woman and taught me the proper way to treat a lady."

It certainly wasn't as easy to confront Kate about her want of propriety.

"I have spent my life being the proper Katherine Grovenor, and if I choose on occasion to go against the rules, damn the consequences," she had cried. "I have only a little time to be with Nick. Don't deny me a little innocent happiness."

She had stormed off, and Slayton knew beyond a shadow of a doubt that Kate was as much, if not more, in love with Nick than he had feared. He owed it to Kate to tell her what he knew about Nick's past and help her over her misery, but he knew she would hate him for being the bearer of such news and all its ramifications for a future together. In time she'd learn how impossible marriage to Nick was, and he would be there to pick up the pieces, if only she would let him.

The pleasure begun when Maitland complimented Kate and Nick on the closely reasoned argument for changes in the laws and conditions of transportation, began giving way to inner turmoil for the three of them.

For Kate and Nick the final document was the greatly lamented end to long hours of work and an excuse to be closeted alone, notwithstanding a compliant maid sitting outside the slightly opened door.

Wanting Nick by her side was no longer enough. She was as naive about men and the mechanics of love and marriage as any schoolroom chit, but a week alone with Nick had given Kate the mother wit to recognize at last that she wanted him to hold her, to touch her, to do whatever men do to women to satisfy the ache she felt in the recesses of her womanhood.

She was moved to inexplicable feelings springing from what she assumed were the secrets of inherited memory. All her fears of being unable to give and accept love made her want to laugh out loud and tell the world how wrong she had been. She wanted to be awakened, if that was the word, and she wanted it now! She wanted it to be Nick who aroused her to the rites of love between a man and a woman. She would pay gladly whatever the price, take whatever the punishment that meant. One hour in his arms would last her years. And if he returned her love, she would have heaven on earth.

Kate looked over at Nick, willing her need of him leap the space that separated them in the carriage. But his chiseled profile, his dark eyes, steely and focused elsewhere, revealed nothing, making a terrible mockery of everything she hungered for, wanted from him.

She was ashamed. She had to get out of the carriage and put room between herself and Nick, or she wouldn't answer for the consequences. Nothing about Nick suggested that he had any more on his mind that Maitland's kind reception of the hours of effort on the report they wrote together. If Nick gave one thought to her as anything more than an agreeable tutor and secretary of sorts, if he returned the slightest feeling that she had for him, she had never seen it. And goodness knows, she was always looking for some sign of deep affection toward her.

With their heads and hands never more than a few inches away, Nick never once seemed to want to touch her or appeared in the least aware of her as a desirable woman. Not once. How she envied the woman who had stolen Nick's heart before she met him. As much as Kate wanted to hate the woman, she couldn't. She could only hope that her rival, if she dared use the word, would love him, care for him, and want him as much as she did. The hopelessness of her infatuation reared up and threatened to choke her.

"Mr. Monroe, please stop the carriage." Kate's tone was peremptory, and, refusing all offers of help, she and her maid were away before they could stop them. The carriage moved on, the men puzzled by Kate's odd departure.

"What happened?" Nick said, unhappy that she would not hear his good news. "I was going to tell Lady Katherine my mother is expected here in a week."

Charlie nodded absently, his thoughts concerned with Kate's strange behavior. He could find no reason why she had demanded to be put down so unexpectedly.

"I am hoping you and she will join us when we go down to Delacourt House over the weekend."

Charlie roused himself.

"I am, of course, delighted by your news, old boy," Charlie said quietly. He loathed being the bearer of unhappy tidings and reminders. "We have both forgotten that Kate's betrothal will be announced soon, and she will have little time to continue her jaunts with us."

Nick groaned. He knew, of course, but he had chosen to forget the time when Kate would no longer be part of their wonderful threesome.

Chapter Fourteen

The door of Kate's sitting room swung open with force sufficient to send it flying against the white-and-yellow-striped wall. The sight of her father, and the reason the door was rocking on its hinges, John Peterbroome, sent her heart down to her shoes.

"In the weeks I have allowed you to think about marrying me, you have done nothing but make a fool of me," Peterbroome said, his normally sallow face red as fire, his thin mouth bared and showing rotting teeth. "I hear of your carousing all about the town with your profligate cousin and that foreign oaf. This will stop at once."

Kate felt the first real terror of her life. She had succeeded in keeping the thought of a future shared with Peterbroome to the edges of her mind, but as reality struck, she stepped back against an antique French armoire to hide the state of her nerves.

"How dare you make such a thunderous and uninvited invasion of my sitting room?" Kate said, fighting for the appearance of defiance she didn't in the least feel. "I have weeks left. If you both want a favorable reply, leave this room at once."

"John is correct," her father said in a tremulous voice, crouching against the door. "We must have your answer."

"Answer be damned," Peterbroome said, raking Pearson Grovenor with seething, bloodshot eyes. "The wedding date is two months off, and that's final. My grandfather is delighted."

He let out a laugh of triumph and bolted from the room, leaving Kate and her father in stunned silence. His boots and spurs jangled down the stairs and the front door closed like thunder a moment later.

"No!" Kate screamed at her father. "I will not marry that fiend, and you can't make me."

Ashen, Pearson Grovenor looked at Kate, started to speak, turned, his shoulders bent, and left the room.

Kate closed the door and leaned against it, her legs leaden weights that wouldn't hold her long enough to reach the safety of the big welcoming bed in the next room. Almost more than her own agony, she was stunned by the state her father was reduced to. She had seen him in every mood of arrogance, but never stricken, old, and careworn. Could her father be as reluctant as she was herself? If so, there was hope for her, if only she could find the right words.

Kate started to go to him, but her own strength was gone, and she found she couldn't navigate the stairs. Her legs gave way, and she slipped to the floor and wept until, mercifully, sleep took over.

"Lady Katherine, it's late," her maid called out, at the same time trying to pry open the door. "Your father and Lord John expect you to accompany them within the hour."

Dazed, Kate needed a moment to remember why she was asleep on the floor. Rousing herself with difficulty, holding back the memory of the afternoon, she stood and admitted the maid. She turned her eyes away from the young Irish lass, afraid she would see her swollen eyes. The girl helped her undress, and Kate followed her on wooden legs to the hot bath awaiting her in the dressing room. Later she would have need of the arts of some makeup to deceive her friends.

An hour later, once again the lady actress, Kate descended the wide, steeply pitched stairs of Grovenor House to find her father and Peterbroome playing cards in the drawing room. Angrily Grovenor threw in his hand, and extracting a bulging chamois bag from a pocket in his yellow brocaded coat, flung it furiously on the table.

"Damn your luck," her father growled, downing the con-

tents of a brimming wineglass. He pulled himself to his feet
and reeled past Kate, cursing all the way to the front door.

Peterbroome scooped up the bag greedily before bothering to acknowledge Kate's appearance. Then his piercing,
red-rimmed gray eyes looked lasciviously at the ivory silk
and lace ball gown cut provocatively low in a square neck-
line, the Grovenor sapphire and diamond tiara glowing like
fireflies on her dark red hair, a matching necklace at her
throat.

"You are still not precisely to my taste, but Grandfather
thinks you'll do, and for the moment, you high-and-mighty
Kate, that is all that is important." He took her arm roughly,
and together they left the house.

The coach, rattling in the tempestuous rain taking them
to Carlton House and a party given by the Prince Regent,
was so full of anger and frustration that Kate could almost
feel it through her gloved hands.

Pearson Grovenor murmured oaths under his breath, and
Peterbroome stared moodily out of the windows, though
what he could see in the impenetrable darkness, Kate could
not imagine.

For herself, she felt only the numbness of defeat. What
she thought was her father's sympathy for the hell he
helped create for her held little consolation. Kate had never
dreamed her father was a coward or afraid of any man. Yet
the events of that afternoon and evening pointed to craven
capitulation to Peterbroome. How strange. How terrible for
both of them.

As if that weren't puzzling enough, there was Peterbroome's freely given admission that he didn't want to
marry her any more than she wanted to marry him. All she
knew about Peterbroome's grandfather was that he was a
tartar of the first water, a hermit hoarding his riches in the
wild fastness of Scotland. The tyranny of old age and
money were a formidable combination, and she wished she
could find it in her heart to feel sorry for John Peterbroome.

All at once Kate felt an explosion of blind fury. How
dare three men determine her fate as if she were a prime
heifer, pulled apart at the whim and will of these creatures,

who wanted her hide, her milk, and, yes, by God, her young. Soon what was on her mind was on her tongue.

"Why me?" she threw out in the bleak silence of the coach. "Why do you want to marry me, John, when it's clear you and I can't abide each other?"

Peterbroome laughed, a frightening, wicked sound it was, and it chilled Kate to the marrow.

"That's an unseemly and terrible question for a maiden lady to ask," her father interposed before Peterbroome could reply.

"Ask your father, my pet," he said, ordering the coachman to stop, hefting the bag holding the gold sovereigns from hand to hand. "I think my luck is in tonight. I shall join you after I multiply this at Brooks. Prinny won't notice my absence."

Peterbroome leaped easily from the moving carriage and was gone.

Kate turned to her father, squirming at her side, as the carriage moved on.

"Tell me. What is this all about? Surely I have a right to know."

"Never."

They arrived on the word and were led from the porte cochere up the commanding staircase to a master of ceremonies in red coat and white knee breeches, who announced their arrival.

The portly, overdressed Prinny, for all the world looking like the jovial host of a prosperous posting house, greeted them lavishly. His eye for a pretty woman was well served with Kate, and he held her hand a little too long. Only a reminder from a sharp-eyed courtier that others were waiting to be presented made the Regent release her hand.

"That was well done, Kate," her father whispered as they entered the ballroom. "Too bad John wasn't here to see it."

Her father's sudden change of mood gave Kate a reason to hope.

"Can't you tell me, Papa, why you need this match?" Kate asked plaintively.

"I hope you never learn," he said, making haste to join a

group of friends across the room, leaving Kate standing by herself.

For the rest of the night, between dances with men whose faces she forgot as soon as the music stopped, Kate wandered from one stifling opulent and overfurnished huge room to another and from one chattering group to another. It was a useless search for the only face and figure that meant anything to her. Nick Monroe. The only man who made her heart want to beat, her body vibrate with a need she couldn't describe, and set her senses reeling at the thought of him. But he was nowhere in sight. Charlie and the Maitlands and Brownings were not to be found either. She felt alone and adrift and impatient for the proper moment to make a quiet departure.

"Leaving without me?" the hated voice jarred against her ears. Would he ever stop stealing up behind her, making her skin crawl and throwing her off her stride?

"And I almost succeeded," Kate said, trying to brush Peterbroome aside.

His hooded eyes burned into her, more threatening than ever, and he was reeling drunk.

Kate suspected he'd lost the heavy sack of gold won earlier from her father, and wasn't surprised. Hadn't she seen her father in the same state after a disastrous night of gaming, railing at the Fates and at the desertion of Lady Luck?

Peterbroome took her by the arm and drew her toward the dance floor.

"You'll learn to monitor that acid tongue once I have control of you, and no mistake." His liquored breath, hot and fetid against her face, sent Kate's head spinning.

"Shall I take it that you lost the money you won from my father?" A bolt of courage shot through her. She was not going to be cowed easily, no matter what the provocation.

"What I win or lose or how I live my life will never concern you. Make no mistake," Peterbroome spat out, stumbling against her.

"You are quite right, since I have no intention of marrying you."

Kate struggled free of his arms and, making quite sure

she was seen by the other guests, stalked off the dance floor without a backward look. He would have to learn once and for all time, she was not going to take his torment lightly.

Chapter Fifteen

Once again the door of Kate's sitting room swung open like a gale. Her father, his heavy, red silk robe flapping behind him like the wings of a maddened bat, came in waving a letter.

"You damn fool, you are ruining me," Grovenor shouted, just as a footman was placing a breakfast tray on the table next to her.

"These dramatic entrances are becoming all too much, Papa," Kate said, rising from her chair.

With her long red hair tied back by a white ribbon, Kate looked vulnerable and lovelier than ever, making Pearson Grovenor stop. Struck by his daughter's fresh and innocent beauty, he fell heavily into a chair.

"You must not go about upsetting Peterbroome in this way," he said, his voice suddenly losing its rage, the words more like a plea. "He said you made a fool of him last night at the ball, and he won't have it."

"What has happened? Tell me."

"He's badgering me again. I can't bear it anymore."

"He's changed his mind about marrying me?" Kate held her breath. She had won.

"Far from it. He wants to advance the date."

Pearson Grovenor looked over at Kate, his lips moving without sound.

"What hold has this animal over you? Tell me," Kate pleaded. She could see her father's moment of frail humanity shatter.

"How dare you suggest anyone has influence over me."

His rage resumed, he sprang from the chair and started to leave.

Kate ran after him and threw herself against the door, barring the way.

"I will not marry John Peterbroome. I can't."

Her father stared at her blindly.

"Then you sound my death knell."

Chapter Sixteen

Rarely had the mid-morning riders and saunterers in Hyde Park seen Kate's like.

Mounted on a charging black stallion, her groom left in the dust, she twice circuited Rotten Row as though the Furies were after her. No amount of weeping or inducement would move her father to explain himself. He had taken refuge in his book room and ordered her away when she tried once more to force him to explain why he lived in such abject fear of Peterbroome.

"Poppy," she begged, using her childhood name for him, "if you are in trouble, tell me. I will try to understand."

But her father was resorting to the comforts of a brandy decanter, his hand and body shaking like the ague.

"I've said all I'm going to say."

Kate could see her father was determined to erase all traces of the fleeting humanity he displayed to her again.

"If you continue in your opposition to this marriage, I will confine you to your bedroom or the country until your wedding day," he said bitingly, the liquor beginning to have effect.

Kate was in no doubt that her father would do exactly as he threatened. She was continually a thorn in his side. She returned to her room, dressed in her riding habit, and left the house too overwrought to remain indoors.

Now panting for breath, as winded as her horse, Kate slowed the pace. In the distance she caught a glimpse of a horse and rider galloping toward her, a magnificent blending of man and beast.

The sight of Nick Monroe riding a prize horse, dressed in

the clothes that made him more than the equal of any aristocrat she had ever known, made her realize that he was the only one who could relieve the funk she was in. She stopped to wait for him to join her.

"Are you feeling better?"

The question told Kate that Nick had been watching and guessed the state of her feelings. She nodded. To speak would have given herself away. Besides, what concern could Nick Monroe have with her? She had served her purpose. Hadn't she introduced him to the best tailor, boot, and hat makers in London? His horses and carriages were the best that Tattersall's had on offer. Of course, she and Charles couldn't take all the credit. It wasn't only the clothes, the fine new haircut from Bond Street, the superb cattle that made Mr. Nicholas Monroe of Delacourt House a welcome addition to every drawing room he deigned to grace.

She knew only too well that Nicholas Monroe was, from the beginning, his own man, and that made him a gentleman. His honesty, energy, and male vigor, all the things she loved about him, surrounded him like an aura. What further use could she, a worn-to-cinders and to her mind faded London ballroom fixture, be to the latest London Nonpareil? Kate gave her horse leave to move forward, while she searched for something to say.

"You seemed to be busy elsewhere and absent from the parties I have attended the last few days," Kate heard herself babble. *There I go, giving away my search at every place I have been this week hoping for a sign of the man who murders my sleep and gives me the most inexplicable dreams.* Just thinking about them made her heart pound in strange ways. What was wrong? Where had all her detachment gone? Overwhelmed, Kate scarcely heard Nick talking to her.

"I have tried to call on you, but I have been turned away, and my flowers spurned at the door," Nick said, hoping he sounded offhand. He was desperate not to show how much he had been hurt by what he thought was her abandonment. "I assumed your butler didn't approve my choice of flowers, which Charlie tells me must be of the right sort or one can make a terrible gaffe."

Kate couldn't believe her ears. Was this the first sign of her father's and Peterbroome's opening moves to wreck her friendships and control her existence? She couldn't allow them to succeed. She needed to be wise. The great aloof, independent Kate Grovenor a pawn of her father and Peterbroome forever? Kate turned a bright and, she hoped, brittle face to Nick. She had nothing more to give him or anyone except the pretense of her former self. No one must know her shame.

"How remiss of me not to have instructed you about flowers," Kate said flirtatiously, or at least she hoped she sounded that way. "It occurs to me that I didn't tell you about calling cards that must certainly accompany the flowers either. If you deliver them yourself, do remember to turn down the top left-hand corner ever so small. But if you decide to send a servant, the right corner, of course, must be turned down. You did include your card?"

Nick was furious and read Kate wrong. He might not be adept at all the social graces, but he could play her game. If Kate had lost interest in him, and it seemed she had, then he would take it for what it was. Dismissal.

"How gauche of me, Lady Katherine," he said tartly. He did not like this Kate as much as he loved the one he thought he knew. "You are always so instructive. How will I flourish without your social superiority and guidance after your marriage?"

And how could I have been so wrong about you? Nick asked himself. How could I have missed your shallowness? How could I have forgotten what a consummate actress you are? What role are you playing now, supercilious London beauty, tired so soon of the hulking colonial and his overweening pretensions? Are you finished with me, Kate Grovenor?

"You must remember, one can't be successful without the aid of these rules of polite conduct," Kate went on mockingly. "Flowers have a language all their own."

"Do they really?" Nick asked, unable to believe he was

actually playing the mindless dandy with, of all people, the woman who could make him supremely happy or only supremely miserable. If he had the wit he was born with, he would drag her off her horse and take her in the bushes and kiss her until her ears rung, or turn around and run for his life. He knew he would do neither, or not at the moment anyway. She had him in thrall, and no mistake, and he kept up his part of the charade, as much as he hated it.

"Do tell me all about flowers, Lady Kate. It would seem that I am as ignorant of those as I am of so many things."

The irony wasn't lost on Kate, even if she didn't understand all that it meant. Blast the subject of flowers.

"Most importantly, yellow flowers mean the end of friendship or dislike. Pink flowers indicate that the giver wishes the recipient to know he has warm feelings and hope of a closer relationship." Kate raced through the recital, embarrassed for allowing herself to fall into such a stupid quagmire. "Now, white flowers may be given under all circumstances. And red roses are very specific. They are made and given for love. They are sent to a lady who is admired by a gentleman, one who lives in hope of love reciprocated."

And what did you send me, my beloved Nick? She would never have the courage to ask. Go away now, please, Nick. If you don't, I will throw myself at you. Here and now I'll lay my head against your chest, and beg you to take me away from the hell being prepared for me.

However much Kate wanted to abandon herself and ask his help, she knew her pride would not allow her. She needed to summon all the strength she could muster to confront her father and Peterbroome. It was past all endurance that they should take secret control of her destiny and try to separate her from the people she loved. If they succeeded, where would it end? A prisoner for life!

Nick couldn't believe the end of his dream had come so cruelly and so soon, and in a bloody park at that. He would survive somehow knowing her marriage to Peterbroome was inevitable, but was he to believe that Kate was not at all different from the other women in London who seemed to want to know him, to be amused by this new toy in their midst. Indeed, some of the most prominent men in the many clubs and places Slayton had taken him didn't scruple to tell him they were instructed on pain of death to issue invitations to him. Until that moment, Nick had felt neither flattered nor tempted. Kate had captured his heart and soul and was all the woman he wanted. What an idiot he was. His mouth was grim. There were a hundred women he could have, and all he wanted was a woman who couldn't stand the sight of him.

They walked their horses, each lost to the signs that might have bridged the gulf opening between them.

"I was hoping that you might like to meet my mother and visit Delacourt House," Nick said, preparing to take his leave. In a last toss of the dice he said, "But I suppose you are taken up with so many other and newer excitements. We would not like to offend."

Nick was turning his horse to leave when racing hooves sounded behind them.

"You are becoming de trop, Monroe," Peterbroome shouted over the noise and dust he created around them. "Lady Katherine is my fiancée, and your attentions are too marked and do not please me."

Kate raised herself in her stirrups and glared fire at Peterbroome. "You presume too much, sir."

"Do I?" he said, steel behind the negligent, la-de-da voice. "Apparently you have not read the announcement of our betrothal in the *Gazette* this morning."

Her engagement was announced! All London now knew what she had tried to keep from them. She had to get hold of herself. It would not do for Peterbroome to see her distress. He could smell weakness a mile away.

Kate smiled beguilingly at Nick and held out her hand.

"Good day, Mr. Monroe. I shall be delighted to meet your mother and visit you both at Delacourt House," she said easily. "I have a school friend nearby who will have me, I am sure. Tell me when it will be convenient, and please be assured that this communication will be received without incident." She thanked her lucky stars she was, above all else, a better actress than she knew.

Nick wasn't sure how to accept Kate's sudden turnabout, until he understood what she was trying to tell him. She hadn't known about his visits or his flowers. She wasn't through with him after all.

Kate continued to look at him, willing him to leave her alone with Peterbroome. Nick kissed her hand and sadly rode off.

"How dare you insult Mr. Monroe?" Kate glowered. "I will have my own friends and my own life. Remember that."

Kate knew she was throwing down the gauntlet, and was suddenly exhilarated. She would fight for her freedom.

If there was to be a marriage between them, it was imperative to start as she meant to go on.

Her voice was cold and expressionless, her eyes daggers. "You have as much as admitted to me that your grandfather wants this marriage and an heir. There will be neither if you continue to hound me and try to restrict my life. I will not be dominated."

Peterbroome's face flushed, and it told Kate all she wanted to know. Her threat, inspired by sheer terror, hit the mark. The key was Peterbroome's grandfather. She wasn't completely without resources, and she would press them for all they were worth. Feeling better, Kate set to leave the park.

"Don't press me too far, Kate," Peterbroome warned. "My grandfather has only limited influence on me, and I will not tolerate a contentious wife."

"Won't you?" Kate tossed her head triumphantly, her hair flowing behind her dashing blue velvet riding hat. She wasn't going to dilute her first moment of triumph over him. The first sign of fear or weakness, both of which hovered over her still, and Peterbroome would trample her in the dirt.

Nick watched the spirited exchange from afar. He wanted nothing more than to pummel Peterbroome into the ground. He forgot Kate's earlier behavior as soon as she promised to come to his house. She might have accepted just to annoy Peterbroome, but he didn't care. He would put up with anything to have Kate at Delacourt, however brief it was to be.

"My heart won't stand all this bother over this damned marriage," her father hissed out of the corner of his mouth that night.

He had just taken his seat at the play, white-faced and shaken after another acrimonious interview with Peterbroome. She ignored him, reluctantly returning the greetings from friends and acquaintances surrounding them in the theater. Despite pleas from her father and Peterbroome, Kate had refused to leave her small gilt chair, knowing everyone would try to wish her well on her engagement. Even her dramatic gifts were not strong enough to accept and return the false felicitations with falsity of her own. She knew many people would think she was mad to enter into marriage with John Peterbroome. And how she agreed with them.

Kate had wept and begged to stay home, but her father and Peterbroome threw tantrums, and it was at last easier to acquiesce.

Her father bent over her.

"The two of you are like fire and water, and I am heartily sick of it," her father whispered. "He's determined to have you, and the sooner you accept it, the better."

"The better for whom?" Kate asked, her voice rising enough to make heads turn toward them.

"Keep your voice down," her father ordered.

"Tell her the truth." Peterbroome arrived and placed his beringed fingers on Kate's shoulder, squeezing hard enough to make her cry out.

Kate's father leaped to his feet, threw a venomous look at Peterbroome, and fled.

"I do seem to have a talent for upsetting you Grovenors, don't I?" Peterbroome chortled, moving to kiss Kate on the neck.

"You are a right bastard, you are," Kate said, going to follow her father.

Chapter Seventeen

Vivian Monroe had been living at Delacourt House for a fortnight, but still she could not walk into a room without touching the walls admiringly or adjusting a picture, checking for dust, nor descend the intricately carved, magnificently restored stairs without feeling a rank intruder.

What was she doing with servants at her elbow anxious to serve her, masses of clothes and jewels fit for a queen, and a bedroom ten times the size of the hovel she and Nick had called home until he came back from the ends of the world a rich man? All this luxury made her head spin.

Here she was, by her own reckoning, a tall, spare, heavily wrinkled woman of five and fifty, standing in the great hall waiting to pour tea for the daughter of one of the premier families of England. She couldn't take it all in, especially when Nick told her that morning that Lady Katherine Grovenor was staying with a school friend nearby and wanted to see the place.

Is it any wonder, she sniffed, that my hands are shaking, my legs feel like treacle pudding, and I'd rather be a world away?

Nick sensed her bewilderment.

"Are you happy, Mam?" he asked, taking her in his arms and rumpling her wiry gray hair just as he had done as soon as he grew enough to tower over her.

"It's smile, cry, or run away," Mrs. Monroe said, standing on tiptoe to kiss his cheek. "Nick, darling, I have forgotten so much of my party manners. Do let me go to my room," she begged. "I am not a skilled hostess, and Lady

Katherine will recognize it at once and think me a jumped-up cow."

"You'll love her," Nick said easily, trying not to show his mother, who could always read him, the depth of his ardor for Kate.

As much as you do, Vivian Monroe wanted to ask, but knew better. She had shrewdly guessed that if this was a shared love, Nick would have told her the moment she arrived in England.

"If she is anything like her cousin, of course I will," Mrs. Monroe said, recovering quickly. Nick in love. It was a shock.

Vivian Monroe leaned her head against her son's chest in silent sympathy. Knowing how he felt about Lady Katherine, she began to understand some of the subtle changes that had taken place in Nick since he arrived in England. She was too wise and too sensitive to this big, giving son of hers not to know that the changes were profound. What she hadn't known was the cause of the difference.

She recognized the changes as more than the air and carriage of a gallant, the superbly cut clothes and fine accouterments. For one thing, the perfect speech was much more pronounced than all her efforts had produced. They may have had to live under primitive, cruel, and hateful conditions, but she had drummed into her son the need for a good accent and command of all the gentler things of life. It had been a never-ending struggle to keep Nick from being scarred forever by the hard experiences of men, women, and children transported to what often seemed the end of the civilized world. That she had succeeded in helping to make him a kind and upright man was a source of great pride. Nick's subsequent success did not surprise her. Ambitious and single-minded from boyhood, Nick was driven by a desire to give her a good life and buy his father's release from the bestial farmer who treated him worse than an animal. Vivian never doubted that Nick would have his way. But she had never imagined how rich he would become. He had succeeded in making her comfortable, but

Nick's riches came too late to help his father. It was a blight she and Nick would always regret.

Nick brought her back to the moment.

"I hear a carriage," Nick said, excitement written on his face. He reached for her and led her toward the great door, his arm around her shoulder.

It was mother and son, arms entwined, that greeted Kate, her maid, and Charlie as her friend Joanna Lyon's landau brought them down a recently renewed avenue of magnificent oak trees.

"Could you imagine a scene like that with your mother?" Charlie asked.

"And you with your mother?" Kate challenged him.

"The last time my mother held me, I was probably five minutes old, and then probably because her old nurse shamed her into it. She was always trying to make her show affection."

Kate was ravishingly beautiful, just as Mrs. Monroe dreaded.

"Welcome to Delacourt House, Lady Katherine," Mrs. Monroe said, taking care to give just the right air of deference without presumptuous familiarity. Vivian hadn't forgotten one iota of the manners her own mother had drummed into her as a girl and she had learned as a governess in this very house.

The older woman didn't know how much Kate Grovenor knew about the Monroe family. Only the barest outlines, she was sure. Whatever the outcome between Kate and her son, she hoped she would not be the one to tell Lady Katherine the seamier side of Monroe family history. It went against her strong character and adherence to the truth to lie about anything. She relied on her son to do the right and proper thing, and if he didn't, she would have something to say.

London may have changed greatly, but she was certain polite society had not. Money and Nick's natural charm, with the added help of Kate and Charlie Slayton, may have opened difficult doors, but it would take an extraordinary

titled Englishwoman to accept the skeleton in her closet of
a man the government and courts had branded a thief.

"Tea must be ready," Mrs. Monroe announced, beckoning her guests into the half-completed drawing room. A
hearty repast of sandwiches, jams and puddings, assort-
ments of cakes and breads were spread before them. If she
expected a moment or two of awkwardness, she found none
at all. Lady Kate was an easy guest, eating with uncon-
cealed gusto, open and friendly, appreciative of everything
set before her. Mrs. Monroe found none of the affected
manners and sides so many of the women of Quality
showed her when she had been at Delacourt House as a
governess before her marriage. If Kate was putting on a
masterly performance of the happily slumming aristocrat, it
escaped her.

Before the tea was half over, Mrs. Monroe understood
completely why Nick was hopelessly in love with Kate. But
why, oh why, had he succumbed to a woman who could not
return his love? There was nothing in Kate's demeanor that
suggested she saw in Nick anything more than an amiable
friend. She could see no sign of virginal blushes and covert
glances. Good. Time would heal Nick's heart, but not before a great deal of pain. She knew about broken hearts.
None better. Vivian Monroe never got over her husband's
transportation and death, and all of her son's riches could
not moderate her grief.

"How marvelous this room is," Kate exclaimed, leaving
her chair with teacup and saucer in hand to move from picture to picture, admiring the new and refurbished country
furniture that captured her special admiration.

"How wonderful to sit in a drawing room that is not
French or German, so delicate one is afraid to stare, or so
heavy that one is oppressed by massiveness," Kate said. "I
prefer sturdy country styles to all else."

"I see you and Nick agree on such matters," Mrs. Monroe said, wondering what else they shared.

"Actually, Mother, Lady Katherine influenced me without
knowing it." Nick laughed. "On our visits to Ackermann's

and Harding, Howell, she helped me form my taste in furniture and decoration. I hope she will help me in the future."

Kate blushed, continuing her study of the room.

"I think Lady Katherine should be taken to see the rest of the house and grounds before she leaves," Mrs. Monroe urged, signaling Charlie to remain. She needed to be alone with him.

When the door closed behind them, Mrs. Monroe invited Charlie to sit beside her on the sofa.

"You know, of course, that Nick is hopelessly in love with your cousin."

"Hopelessly," Charlie agreed. "But I fear Nick didn't tell you that Kate is engaged to be married shortly."

"No. I think he has been to shy to tell me anything about Lady Katherine. I suspect love is all on Nick's side."

Charlie moved from the sofa to the window. Did he dare tell Mrs. Monroe what only he knew?

"Lord Charles, tell me what you seem afraid to say." Mrs. Monroe urged. She wanted to know everything.

"Kate is as much in love with your son as he is with her," Charlie said, turning around to face her. "Neither Kate nor Nick knows how the other feels. I beg you to keep my secret. It would be sinful to give them hope. Forgive me for saying this, but a marriage between them will never happen. It isn't politic, you see."

Mrs. Monroe nodded vigorously. "I share your feelings. Did Nick tell you that I was a governess and met his father here in this very house? His father worked for the family's solicitor."

Slayton shook his head.

"I know a lot about the good and bad aristocracy," Mrs. Monroe said, almost talking to herself. "I never had any desire to imitate my betters, and just as well. Forgive me, but the Quality can be very cruel if they think a member of the lower orders has ambitions above her station. I don't want Nick hurt, and will fight the very devil himself to save him from himself."

Charlie knew exactly what Mrs. Monroe meant. Hadn't he seen the truth of it all his life?

"He must not count too heavily on the splash he made in London," Nick's mother went on, her voice a flood of sarcasm. "My son may be the latest nine-day wonder, but when the truth of his origins comes out, he will be ostracized. It will take two generations for the *ton* to forgive him and his descendants."

"But society women throw themselves at his feet, and their husbands shower him with invitations," Charlie protested. "I've seen it, and been surprised myself."

"These are married women. They are safe. And it is London," she said, in what could only be described as her former governessy way. "Your London high flyers are always looking for the latest bear who walks on hind legs. In the country, your sort are far more hidebound and conservative. Even if he owns and improves Delacourt House, any hint of scandal and they will freeze him out of their circle. And you know it."

Yes, Charlie did know how his family and friends treated outsiders. Sometimes he felt himself like an outsider. Together he and Mrs. Monroe looked gloomily through the windows over the undulating lawns, lost in their own less than joyful memories.

This is the penalty for hubris, Vivian Monroe was thinking. Had I not filled Nick's head with my love of Delacourt House, he would not have dreamed of owning it and seeing me preside as mistress. She had protested vigorously when he said he would try to buy the estate, afraid the old scandal would come to life again.

But Nick was never easily dissuaded from any course he decided on. She did not care for society. All Nick had wanted for her and himself was the opportunity to lead a life of ease and grace in pastoral surroundings. But that was before Nick lost his bearings and fell in love. Lady Katherine had a lot to answer for, Mrs. Monroe thought, clenching her fists.

Now that they were alone, Kate hastened to apologize to Nick for her behavior when they last met in Hyde Park.

"I had your note, Lady Kate," Nick said. "I prefer to forget the whole incident, especially as you are now here and I can show off my home."

Kate was delighted not to have to explain, and she fell in step beside Nick. They went from room to room. Few were altered, and many were still in ruin, and Kate kept a running commentary as they walked.

"Hang about, Lady Kate," Nick implored. "I can't remember all your ideas and suggestions."

"You don't have to," she said, her voice young and carefree, London, her future, and Peterbroome far away. "I have a good memory for details, and shall make sketches and send them to you as soon as I return to my friend's house."

Having Kate to himself after more than a week's absence was heaven, but seeing her in his house—which he wanted more than anything to be her house—was almost more than he could bear. Every purchase was made with Kate in mind. Would she like this addition? Would she approve all his plans for the house? Nick knew he was courting heartbreak having Kate beside him now, but he wouldn't have it otherwise. At least in the coming years—barren years to be sure—he would have the memory of her in every room they wandered. If he had nothing else, he would have those. They were a cold comfort to be sure, but he didn't care. Kate was flesh and blood near him now.

They came to the long gallery, now free of Delacourt family portraits, the walls showing white and desolate where they once hung, cold, haughty, and dead, Kate was sure.

"What are your plans for the gallery?" she asked, turning around to hear his reply. Close behind her, Kate's sudden movement took Nick by surprise, and they collided. She was near enough for him to feel her breasts brushing against him. His breath caught in his throat, and his arms began encircling her. The hell with caution and wisdom, but it was an instant aberration, and Nick dropped his arms. He turned away, every nerve in his body shaking, his need to hold, to touch, to feel this woman who excited him with desire. He wanted her. Denial was purgatory.

Nick was unable to look at Kate, afraid he would see shock and disgust in her face.

He rattled on. "I was going to ask you to recommend a portrait artist who would paint my mother and me," he said, hoping his voice didn't betray him, leading the way out of the gallery and down the famous carved staircase.

A minute before he had not even thought of the portraits, and yet it was a very good idea. The beginnings of a Monroe dynasty were surely worthy of a place on the empty gallery walls. He was delighted.

"I will supply you the names of several very good artists," Kate was saying in a choked voice, still rocked by Nick's arms around her, however briefly. "I hope you will choose Lady Jane Dantry. She's a delightful, rather fiery young Irish painter new to London. Actually she prefers painting miniatures, but is exceptional in everything she does. She will soon be all the crack, and everyone will sit for her."

She is also quite beautiful and determinedly unmarried, Kate added to herself. *I am jealous of any woman who looks at you, and I am not ashamed to admit it, but only to myself, of course.*

"Has she painted you?" Nick asked, hoping he kept his eagerness well hidden.

"Actually, she did a quick study of me recently, but was not at all happy with the result," Kate explained. "I could not convince her to sell or give it to me. She is most exacting."

"If you give me Lady Jane's direction, I shall call upon her and judge her skill for myself," Nick said easily. In fact, he was impatient and would go up to London as soon as he could to persuade the artist to sell him the sketch or do a miniature of Kate from memory.

Nick's heart was light and hopeful. He might not have Kate herself in the dim future, but he would have her likeness. Small mercies were not to be dismissed so easily.

Kate turned on the stair and looked up at Nick, the last rays of a heavenly summer catching him in an almost over-powering and magical light. Her breath caught in her throat. No man could ever mean so much to her, and he was lost to her forever. Damn her father, and damn Peter-broome.

Nick saw the odd look of wonder succeeded so quickly by an expression of misery. He wanted to wipe away a tear that formed at the edge of her eye. He wanted to ask her why she was so unhappy, when all had been so warm and sweet between them a moment before. He had no right to know her secrets. He had no rights at all. Suddenly the house seemed to close in on him. He needed air, and he needed it badly.

"And now, my dear Lady Kate, I shall show you my gardens," he said, offering his arm, trying to console himself with the promise of having Kate's likeness close to him all his life.

The gardens at Delacourt House were further along in Nick's ambitions for the restoration of the estate than the house itself, he was telling Kate.

"I swear I am going to make this a showplace," Nick added, his eyes keen with a look down the coming years. "I shall respect Capability Brown's designs in all respects, but it is in the farms that I shall make great and important changes."

Kate thrilled at the promise in Nick's deep voice, wanting more than ever to be at his side when he brought his vision for all of Delacourt House to fruition.

"How?" Kate asked softly, afraid her voice would give away her longing to be with him down the years.

"I shall don a laborer's smock and do precisely what the Earl of Leicester did. I shall work alongside my tenants and teach them the latest agricultural methods," Nick said as they walked through orchards and the garden with ancient trees and rolling lawns pruned and reseeded by willing and expert hands. "My annual sheep shearing will be an event of national interest, the way his are."

Even removed as she was from the running of the Grovenor family lands, Kate had heard of Thomas Coke of Norfolk, whose estate, Holkham House, was a model of modern farming. He was the envy of her father and his friends. They compared their low yields and were jealous.

"I've heard that in forty years the earl increased the field at Holkham tenfold," Nick said, his eyes scanning Delacourt's farms in the shadowy distance. "I'm boring you to tears, but I tend to be very single-minded when I have a new interest."

"I am not in the least bored, and can see how you have succeeded so young." Kate laughed, driven to awe by Nick's obvious aspirations to be an important landowner.

"Luck and good men who gave me a leg up helped a lot," Nick said, stooping to retrieve a large crooked limb fallen from a majestic tree near the ornamental lake. He swept it like a scythe before them while they walked about companionably.

"Is that why you helped Charlie?"

"How much has he told you?"

"Everything."

"Charlie's tongue is too big for his mouth." Nick chuckled. Her cousin had a great deal of explaining to do the next time he saw him.

"For your ears only, Lady Kate," Nick said, taking off his coat and spreading it on the newly mowed lawn within sight of the house. He took Kate's hand in his and helped her down.

"I saved an American ship's captain from a pack of villains in Sydney, and took him back to his ship. He was nearly dead," Nick explained painfully. "The second mate, a prissy and frightened man, didn't know what to make of me in my rags, big as I was, a half-starved ten-year-old. When the tide came in, he weighed anchor and let Captain Evans decide what to do with me when he came 'round, if he ever did."

"And no word to your mother?"

"Not for almost a year."

"How terrible."

"It couldn't be helped, believe me. In that letter telling Mam I was alive, there was enough money for her to live decently," Nick said quietly. "By then I knew my future lay in emulating John Jacob Astor. He's an American wizard who bought furs in Alaska and shipped them to China in his own ships. Instead of coming back empty, he loaded them with precious spices. With his profits from all his trading, he bought real estate in New York. I have followed him slavishly."

"You were so young."

"Alaska and China are a young man's game, and I lived and breathed my trade. Never spent a penny that couldn't bring me back twenty. I could read, write, and add a column of figures faster than an abacus, and the Chinese liked that. By the time I was sixteen, they made me and Captain Evans their agents, and I bought part of his ship. We have ten ships now, and are partners to this day."

Kate studied the sylvan charms around them, and said, "With such an exciting life, how can you settle down in a rural village, or is this just a sojourn?"

He weighed his answer.

"I am not afraid of boredom, Lady Katherine," he said, smiling at her. "I've roamed long enough. After I see my mother happily installed here, I shall occasionally visit the Orient and America to see to my holdings, but Delacourt will be my special place. My heart is here."

Kate waited. Surely this was where he would tell her about the woman he loved and his marriage.

Nick knew this was the perfect opportunity to tell Kate how much he loved her, but the words died aborning. Peterbroome might be a fiend, but he was acceptable to Kate's father and the circle that meant so much to all of them. Only the other day, Charlie finally convinced him of the immutable rules of titled marriages. Love was the least asset bargained by family solicitors in the marriage settlements. It was all land, money, and succession.

"The idea, dear boy, is to produce an heir and one to spare. The lady conceives and delivers, God willing, two males in the fastest time possible, and then husband and wife may go their own ways," Charlie said as nonchalantly as if he were talking about breeding horses.

Thinking about it now, Nick struck the branch against his

leg. The callousness of it all still rankled. Where was love in all this?

"What's troubling you, Mr. Monroe?" Kate asked, startling him.

"Nothing. I was remembering a very painful incident. Now let's rejoin my mother and Charlie." With an athlete's grace, he rose and led her toward the house.

Before they arrived, Kate stopped and adjusted her gloves.

"I shall call upon Lady Jane for you in London and tell her to expect you one day," Kate said, offering her hand.

Soon after, Nick and his mother took Kate and Charlie to their carriage.

"What did you think of Lady Kate?" Nick asked, watching his guests depart. "Isn't she quite fabulous?"

His mother didn't answer, leading him determinedly toward the library.

Grim-faced, Mrs. Monroe waited until the butler closed the door behind them. She didn't believe in talking too much before Nick's staff at any time, especially now.

"What's the matter, Mam? Steam is coming out of your ears." Nick laughed.

"You may want to be a London beau and a country squire, but you won't get very far if the servants talk to the neighborhood about what they hear." Vivian Monroe was seething, and she didn't intend to hide it from her son.

"I wondered when you were going to take me to task and reduce me to a little boy again," Nick answered, not nearly as casual as he hoped he sounded.

"What are you playing at, Nicky?" she asked. "And don't insult my intelligence and tell me you're not in love with Katherine Grovenor."

"I am, but I'm fighting it all the way," Nick said wearily.

"Does she share your feelings?" Mrs. Monroe didn't dare use the word love. It seemed too painful in the circumstances.

"Far from it. She thinks of me as simply a friend of Charlie's."

Vivian was delighted. Slayton was right. Nick was in the dark about Kate's feelings for him.

"Charlie tells me Lady Katherine is engaged to be married to a rotter," Mrs. Monroe said cagily. "Does that worry you at all?"

"Desperately," he said angrily. "He's loathsome."

"Are you planning to rescue her?" Mrs. Monroe held her breath.

"Not a hope."

ward the tragic and herself. She was thrilled when he took her seldom speaking before she knew him, even to the guests. When he offered a few kind details of his life from time to time.

Chapter Eighteen

It was an hour before dawn the next morning when Kate, her maid, and Charlie left her friend's house in a traveling carriage with another carrying Slayton's valet close behind them. The ride back to London was long, filled, for Kate, with tender memories and terrible unease about the weeks and years ahead.

By rights, Delacourt House should be mine, Kate told herself, reviving in her head all the rooms she and Nick had wandered in and out of, she making suggestions and he trying to keep up with her. The grounds and his plans for the estate were so wonderful that she could see them as if he had drawn her a picture. She could never question the dictates of her heart and imagination. Life with Nick would be all she ever wanted for herself, and he was a man she would follow to the ends of the earth, if he asked her.

Nick treated her as an equal, a new and heady prospect of what life should be. He listened to her, consulted her when most of the men she knew—with the exception of Tarn and Browning—regarded women with disdain, as lifeless, mindless decorations on their arms. Even the most admired political hostesses fooled themselves if they thought they were taken seriously by the great men of state. If they didn't, Kate knew the truth. It was their money, titles, powerful husbands and lovers, and stately homes that gave these women the cachet needed to attract and bring together equally famous men, those men who ran the English empire.

But Nick seemed to have no such reservations about women, at least from what she could see of his attitude toward his mother and herself. She was thrilled when he told her about his life before she knew him, even if, as she guessed, he had edited a few lurid details about his adventures and misadventures.

Kate was touched beyond words when he volunteered his story, and wanted to tell him about her love of the stage, Herr Hendricks, and the little company she supported. But her natural reticence and fear that he would lose regard for her kept her silent. Could she trust him with her secret? She was afraid to try.

And how she wanted him to admire her. Be truthful, Kate, you want him to love you . . . and make love to you. Kate blushed, unable to deny the vision of herself in bed with Nick. Those long, tapering fingers, roughened by years of hard labor, the length of him on top of her, his marvelous curving lips—the most tantalizing she had ever seen—roaming over her body and making her a real woman at last.

Kate felt a wetness under her breasts, and her thighs tautened, and her heart beat like a hammer on an anvil. She was in turns shocked, dumbstruck, and breathless.

So this is what people mean when they say that love is everything. There was nothing like it, she knew for certain. Is this why her unmarried friends talked endlessly of men, love, and marriage, some so hungry they sought out crafty wiles and nostrums to make a reluctant suitor come up to scratch? Kate had laughed at them. It had all seemed to trivial and useless. And all at once, Kate wanted to have everything other women craved. She wanted Nick Monroe.

All the time she thought her friends were stupid, that the men they craved wanted the chase, the surrender, and time in bed with them, only to forget their existence when it suited them. At least that was what her father seemed to want, and she was sure all John Peterbroome wanted of her.

Kate suspected that what awaited her with Peterbroome would be unmitigated hell.

Alert to the turmoil going on in Kate, Charlie put his arm around her and held her close.

"Darling girl, what is it?"

"I can't marry Peterbroome," Kate whispered. Her maid was fast asleep, but still she must be careful.

It was what Charlie was afraid of and why he had begged Kate not to visit Delacourt House. He knew that seeing Nick and the estate would give Kate ideas and make her more unhappy with her lot.

"Have you an alternative to marrying?" he asked, painfully aware that there were none. She knew it as well as he.

"I could kill myself." She laughed hollowly.

"Don't be daft." Charlie pushed Kate away so that he could study her. "Melodrama doesn't suit you."

"What's one death against another? Marriage to John will be a living death," Kate said finally, breathing hard, determined not to cry. "Even I know his reputation. Not as graphic as surely you do, but enough to know what might be in store for me."

Charlie wanted to protest, but it would be an unconscionable lie. Kate almost certainly faced unrelenting tyranny. In certain circles, Peterbroome was called Satan, and for good reason. He was bad through and through, and only his grandfather's considerable power in the halls of Parliament kept his grandson from jail or the gallows. It was rumored that in one drunken orgy he killed a woman. In other times he'd paid dearly for maiming a prostitute and killing a man outside one of the meanest gambling cribs near the dockyards.

What bothered Charlie the most was knowing that Pearson Grovenor knew even more than he did about Peterbroome. What his uncle knew had to be more than rumors. Grovenor hated the march of time, was the butt of clubdom for the way he sought out younger roisters like Peterbroome, trying to hold back the dawn of old age.

Charlie kept all this from Nick, knowing that the hotheaded Australian would have taken matters in his own hands long before this. He was glad that Monroe was busy at Delacourt House and likely to remain there for some time, with luck until after Kate's wedding.

Charlie reached over and took her hands in silent commiseration.

"Don't fret, Charlie dear. I won't kill myself. I love life too much," Kate said, smiling weakly at him. "I have written to Amy Tide, a cousin of my mother's, asking for shelter. She is a very wealthy and fiercely independent spinster. I am hoping she would risk displeasing Papa, because she hates him as much as he hates her."

Charlie wanted to say that the plan would never work. For men like his uncle and Peterbroome, it would be a challenge they couldn't resist, a deadly chemical for bullies. Kate would be dragged to the altar, and no mistake.

"Would you consider running off to Gretna Green with me, Kate darling?" Charlie spoke so low he was afraid she didn't hear him. He held his breath, stunned by his own temerity. "I have loved you forever it seems."

Kate had known and regretted that she could never return Charlie's feelings for her, but even hopeless as matters stood, she could not accept his offer of rescue. It would be his ruin. He was poorer than she was, despite their fathers' plump pockets, and Charlie could never live in poverty. After all, he'd met Nick in a desperate attempt to avert shame and the deprivations of bankruptcy, risking public disgrace and his life.

She would hate being poor, but it would not defeat her as it would her cousin. If Cousin Amy wouldn't take her in, she might think about the stage as a career, if not in London, then in the provinces. And that was no place for kind, happy-go-lucky-the-embodiment-of-London Charlie Slayton. No, she couldn't accept his sacrifice. Who was she fooling? It wasn't any of the reasons she had just given herself. She wanted no other man in her life except Nick Monroe. It was as simple as that.

Kate patted Charlie's hand and smiled at him with tears glistening in her eyes.

"I love you for asking, but you and I both know it would be a disaster," she said kindly. "Don't worry. I'll come about."

Kate hoped she wasn't whistling in the dark.

Chapter Nineteen

Nick crept into the last row of the stalls.

Kate's henchman, Barkley, was expecting him. He had sent a stable boy with a cryptic note asking for word of Kate's next performance. Nick had received a reply and left immediately for London.

Delacourt House no longer held him without Kate to bring it alive. He had to see Kate and knew in her unhappiness she would seek solace in acting.

Even now Barkley was grudging in his consent, but soon allowed him into the theater on a promise to stay in one place and leave on his signal.

Nick was enthralled. The night's performance was different from the first. There was no orchestra, just a piano, and only Kate occupying center stage playing some of Shakespeare's most famous women. After weeks of seeing the best actresses of the London stage, Nick could see that Kate would soon be their equal. She had the same commanding presence, the liquid flowing movements, the voice that could run up and down a man's spine and make him cry. He couldn't bear that Kate's talent was lost to the world. He felt cheated, just as he was sure she did.

Nick was so moved that he was almost able to forget that the towering Lady Macbeth wiping the blood from her hands, the young, demure Juliet dying for her lost love was, in fact, his own Kate. Lost to him. Nick reared back when Barkley touched him on the shoulder.

"It's time, sir."

Nick followed him from the darkened playhouse and out

into the alley. He tried to give Barkley a tip, but the big man waved it away.

"How is your mistress?" Nick asked, handing Barkley a cigar and taking one himself. It was so much like the first time they met.

Barkley waited for Nick to light the stogie before answering.

"Her maid said there's a deal of arguing between Lady Katherine and the master over that Peterbroome," the servant said, wary and watching Nick's reactions. "She cries a lot, and that ain't the Lady Kate we know."

Nick cursed under his breath.

"Anything else?" Nick knew Barkley was holding something back. "I am Lady Katherine's friend. You know that."

"She's told Mr. Hendricks this is her last performance, and he will have to disband the company."

"There's more, isn't there?"

Barkley walked around as if trying to make up his mind.

"Her maid told me this morning Lady Kate has taken to getting up early in the morning before the house is awake and goes 'round to the moneylenders with bits and pieces of jewelry."

Nick burrowed into his pockets and came out with a guinea, and this time he refused to let Barkley give it back.

"There may come a time when you can't get word to me and need to press someone else into service with a message for me. Understand?"

Barkley took the shiny gold coin and put it in his wide belt.

"What is it you want to know, gov?"

"When Lady Katherine is in trouble. I trust you'll know better than I when that will be."

The servant agreed and returned to the theater.

Nick walked to his rented house on South Audley Street, changed clothes, then went in search of Charlie. He started with White's, and it was a lucky strike. He found his friend watching a tremendously steep game of hazard involving Pearson Grovenor and John Peterbroome playing against each other. A stack of bills and gold piled high were at the center of the table, each man clearly eyeing the pot against the depleted coins and banknotes in front of them. The tension around the table was apparent, if unseen. In time the winnings went to Grovenor, who crowed over his luck.

Seething, Peterbroome stood up and took the card table in two hands and began to overturn it.

"Don't be a fool." Tall and patrician Tarn Maitland, with Browning at his elbow, called from across the room in a manner that was both warning and disgust.

"Mind your own bloody business, you jumped-up bastard!"

Men came running from around the room toward the card table, with others closing ranks around Tarn. The room was coolly quiet. Charlie whispered, "Peterbroome is a deadly shot and a master with a sword."

Nevil Browning was the first to recover, calling out for the servants to bring him a glove. Maitland shook his head.

"There will be no duel in my name. You're a drunken disgrace, Peterbroome, and when I fight you, it will be with a horsewhip for *everyone* to witness."

Peterbroome cursed, slowly lowered the table, and withdrew surrounded by his friends. Maitland and Nevil came over to where Nick and Charlie stood mute, unable to forget what they'd just seen.

"Mr. Monroe, just the man I am looking for. I have an old story I would like to tell you," Tarn said, taking Nick's arm and detaching him from the others, propelling him out of the room.

"A great caliph was displeased with an adviser, and ordered his execution," Tarn said jauntily. "The adviser saw a dog at the foot of the caliph's throne and said if his life was spared, he would teach the dog to speak in a year.

"The adviser told his wife. She thought he was crazy. But the adviser answered. 'Three things can happen in a year: I could die, the caliph could die, or the dog could learn to talk.' "

Nick laughed politely, knowing it applied in some way toward his anguish about Kate and his concerns for his

Australian report. Dare he ask which one? They said Captain Tarn Maitland made miracles. He hoped so.

The sun was coming through the great bowed drawing room windows overlooking the Albany's Italian garden. Nick and Charlie were returning from late supper at Stephen's Hotel after the near disaster at White's earlier in the night.

Already news of the encounter was the prime topic in late-night London, and anyone who witnessed it was an instant celebrity. They could talk of nothing else.

"Charlie, I'm heartily sick of it," Nick said, loosening his cravat, grateful for the deep chair Charlie offered him. "I did, after all, seek to talk to you about something else."

Nick told him that Kate was getting into the hands of the pawnbrokers. In exchange, Charlie told him about the threat Kate made to go to her relative in a tiny hamlet in a remote part of Yorkshire.

"It kills me that she must be the one to run away," Nick said. "The unfairness of all this makes my blood boil."

Charlie poured Nick a drink, and the two sat glumly staring into the fire.

"I may not be able to rescue Kate from Peterbroome myself, but I can make sure she has enough money to elude him and that poor excuse for a father," Nick said, a wild look in his eye.

Charlie shook his head and protested. "Don't interfere, Nick, please. You'll only get hurt."

Nick's temper flared out of frustration, "I will do all I think is necessary to save Kate."

Chapter Twenty

Pearson Grovenor's library was a shambles, looking like a troop of cavalry had charged through. Tables were on end, books littered the floor, pictures tilted and moved on wires like metronomes on the walls.

Bruised and cowering, Grovenor was fending off the final indignity. Lord John Peterbroome stood pounding a riding crop against his side.

"You allowed Maitland to make a fool of me in front of my friends." Peterbroome was screaming and swaying, his voice thick with drink. Peterbroome lifted the crop to strike Grovenor. The door flew open, and Kate stood there horrified.

"Put that down and leave at once, or I will scream down the house and have you thrown out."

Peterbroome dropped his hand and, brushing past Kate without speaking, left the house.

Kate turned to the butler who had come up from his quarters, tying the thick rope belt of his bathrobe, his hair on end, his eyes bulging in wonder.

"Get me some hot water and bandages, Jenkins, please," Kate said, closing the door quickly behind him.

"Be a man, and tell me what this is all about," Kate said determinedly. "What is your death knell after all?" She handed her father a drink. "What do you call what he was trying to do just now?"

Her father seemed to diminish before her eyes. Gone was the strutting, aging Casanova, the bon vivant she was used to seeing. He was more pathetic than ever, an old man. She didn't know what to do. He emptied the heavily etched glass and put it down on the table almost as if it was too heavy to hold.

"I am in his debt, and nothing I have offered him will move him," Grovenor said in a strangled voice. "I did a terrible thing. I cannot even confess it to you."

"Fustian," Kate shouted, her patience at end. "I am your daughter. I know you're not a saint. Tell me, and free both of us from this monster."

"I cheated at cards."

Chapter Twenty-one

Her father, a self-confessed cardsharp! Kate couldn't believe it, didn't want to believe that a man who purported to hold the honor of the family name above everything—her future and her happiness among them—was capable of such a violation of the Gentleman's Code.

When, in the small hours of the night, Kate speculated about what her father had done to accept a discredited roué of Peterbroome's stripe as a son-in-law, cheating was never a consideration. That her father had done something dreadful was a certainty, but what it was eluded her completely.

Glancing over at him now, a shadow of the former hale and hearty blusterer, made Kate want to cry for both of them.

Or laugh. Or both.

Her life was to be ruined because of a stupid card game. Kate paced the room, waiting for the butler to return. She couldn't look at her father again. It was too painful.

Then cold reason took hold. She knew the rules of society as well as anyone. Murder was almost more tolerable among gentlemen of their set, because one could always plead extenuating circumstances, dementia, or self-defense. But for cheating at cards, on a par with failure to pay gambling debts, there were no excuses in the convoluted list of ungentlemanly behavior.

What was worse, word moved fast. The penalty was nothing short of ostracism by friends of a lifetime and the forfeiture of a role in London society and all the fashionable watering holes. It was a tragedy, a form of hell on earth usually enacted in the country, the more remote the better, or exile abroad.

Many men killed themselves, and the thought made Kate stop pacing and look over her shoulder. The sight was terrible. Pearson Grovenor made a pathetic picture, hiding like a fearful child in a massive wing chair beside the dying firelight.

He looked up, saw Kate studying him, and tears streaked down his face. He was a cruel caricature of himself.

"I never thought to bring shame on the Grovenor name."

The name! The name. Always the name. Outraged, Kate rode out the storm brewing in her head by stirring the few coals remaining in the grate with a slashing movement. She couldn't understand. Her father was capable of many things, but Kate couldn't believe he was a cheat. She began to question him.

"I was drunk, and there were witnesses, Kate. Only through John's influence was a scandal averted. Surely you can see I am in his debt forever."

"And payment of that debt is me." Kate laughed hollowly. Her father nodded.

"What I can't understand is why has Peterbroome chosen me, when there are so many others, richer and far more biddable, who wanted to marry him all these years."

"His grandfather specified you by name, and I suspect he was given an ultimatum," Grovenor said. "He knows I would never have accepted him as a son-in-law, if he didn't know my shame. You can see how he loves to torture me about it."

It was at last clear to Kate why Peterbroome did not take offense when she made no secret of her dislike for him in every way she could. He needed the marriage as much as her father needed his silence. The two deserved each other. It was a devil's bargain, if ever there was one. She was in the wrong place at the wrong time. What a joke.

Kate felt a distant door slam shut on all her dreams. Any remote chances of escape and rescue were futile, and she'd known it from the beginning.

There was a knock, and the library door swung open on the butler weighed down with an enormous silver tray laden with the water and bandages she had ordered. If the situation were not so frightful, Kate would have laughed. Jenkins, trying not to look at his master's bloodied face, carried provisions enough for a minor disaster. The man stood about ready to lend his help.

Kate refused his offer of assistance, and sent him to bed. One mercy at least, Kate knew he would not tattle as so many servants did. Besides, Jenkins's continued presence would humiliate her father even more. Rolling up the sleeves of her filmy white nightclothes, Kate went to work patching her father's face as best she could. Years of studying family remedies and nostrums gathered from books while representing her gadabout mother as the real chatelaine of Grovenor Hall, gave Kate's hands skill and quickness. She worked in silence trying to lose herself in the effort.

"Do you hate me?" her father asked pitifully during a pause in her ministration.

More than anything, Kate wanted to tell him all the big and small hurts she had kept hidden since her childhood. She couldn't do it, knowing it might give her momentary satisfaction, but, in the end, she would hate herself.

Kate's world was whirling on its axis, with nothing as it should be. For in many ways this was a night she would remember, when she became the parent, and her father became the errant child. He caused terrible havoc and now wanted only to be forgiven. The man who had loomed so large in her life, strong, proud, imperturbable, despite his selfish, hedonistic ways, was gone forever. There was no joy in losing a parent, whatever the cause.

Kate finished the last of the patchwork and turned to making a sling for her father's right arm. She was certain it wasn't broken, but it was badly bruised and painful. Peter-broome had hit her father with a heavy Ming horse, now in a mound of shards at her feet.

Kate was too tired and dispirited to reply to her father's endless and lame attempts to justify himself. She threw down the scissors and rolled up the bandages. Having done all she could, nature and her father's valet would have to do the rest. Kate managed a tentative smile. After a few days of enforced confinement to the house, her father would be walking the walls and would come up with a plausible reason for looking like he'd met a windmill. She could see him returning to his usual haunts with a cock-and-bull story and resume his pleasures as if nothing happened.

"I ask you again, Kate darling, do you hate me?"

Kate stood at the door, her hand on the knob, preparing to call Jenkins to escort her father to his room.

"No. But from now on there will be changes. I promise you."

It was a far different Kate who awoke at three the next afternoon. She was in the best spirits. Although worn to tears the night before, Kate had not been able to sleep, but the time was far from wasted. She lit a branch of candles always left on the table next to her bed and retrieved her wood and leather lap desk. This was always nearby, kept for such sleepless nights. At other times she was given to drawing ideas for costumes and simple scenery for Herr Hendricks's plans and suggestions for roles she hoped to do in the future. Several pages of foolscap with sketches drawn weeks before were still in the desk. What a simpler time all that seemed now. Then her only concern was being found out in an innocent game of make-believe. How foolish she'd been. Kate rolled up the last reminders of her innocence and pushed them aside.

She wrote notes for hours and made drawings for Delacourt House to add to those she had already sent to Nick. She might never preside over the wonderful old house, but at least she could picture Nick against the setting she had helped create for him. She placed her letters outside her room with orders for her maid to see to their distribution. Tomorrow, after she saw Charlie, she would go to see Jane Dantry about the portraits. A permanent reminder of Nick was uppermost in her mind.

Now awake and anxious to be up and about, Kate rang for tea and toast and stretched and purred contentedly like the laziest cat. An apt thought, since she decided she had several more lives left of the nine accorded the proverbial cat.

The resolutions set in motion the night before were soon in effect and evident. In the middle of her tea, Jenkins asked to be admitted.

"His Lordship and Lord Peterbroome wish to see you at once," the butler reported in stentorian tones, only to add in an aside, "in the restored library, my lady."

"How nice, Jenkins," Kate said, daintily applying a lace napkin to her lips. "I must go out at once. I will return at six and will see them in the morning room for a few minutes."

The butler stared at her, seemingly unable to suppress his surprise.

"Be sure you are very specific, dear Jenkins," Kate said, winking at him.

A few minutes later her father and fiancé knocked on the door and asked for admittance. Kate was pleased to recall other times when the amenities were not observed. Kate laughed, and the sound was like manna. It seemed an age since she'd felt in command of her life.

"What are you playing at again, refusing to see me at once?" Peterbroome said, shoving her father aside at the open door. "Don't try your tricks on me. I am not one of your tongue-tied moonlings, taking your crumbs for stardust."

"How lyrical, dear John," Kate said, knowing she would send him into the alt with the next thing she said. "Father told me the truth about the marriage, and if you want me as your wife, you had better learn to mend your ways. The both of you."

Peterbroome turned on her father, and his rage was plain and ugly. He began to lift his arm toward Grovenor.

"Don't you dare," Kate said in a low, unmistakable threat. "If you touch my father once more, I will make such a hue and cry of breaking off our engagement that your grandfather will hear of it all the way to Scotland."

Peterbroome's arm fell.

"You damned fool," he said, his preternaturally old and wasted eyes staring venomously at Kate and her father.

He pulled out a sheaf of letters from the pocket of his purple riding coat and waved them at her.

"How dare you cancel every request our friends have made to entertain and congratulate us?"

"I don't want congratulations on a travesty," Kate said equably. She had never thought to see Peterbroome, who professed to hate society, so eager for approval. It was something to remember in the future. He was a hypocrite. "You should be happy I didn't explain my real aversion to the invitations, and merely said no."

Peterbroome was clearly knocked out by this new Kate. She pressed the advantage.

"And let me tell you something else that has exercised me for days," Kate added. "I tell you for the last time, you will not bar anyone from this house who wishes to see me or send flowers to me. Is that clear?"

Kate's father and her fiancé exchanged shocked and puzzled glances. She loved it. All their secret maneuverings meant to isolate her were out. She was not going to be their victim any longer.

"Further, I will see my friends as often and as publicly as I like," she added, pulling the servants' cord next to her bed to summon Jenkins. "This is a terrible bargain we are tied to, and if you want to turn me up sweet, respect *my* new rules."

Jenkins appeared quickly. Kate smiled. She knew he heard everything.

Her pleasure was short-lived.

"Get the hell out of here." Peterbroome sprung at the butler and pushed him through the door and closed it with a crash.

"I will not have you mistreat our family servants the way you must mistreat your own," Kate said.

"Your servants be damned, and the same with you and

your fool of a father," Peterbroome bellowed. "I will not have my word or actions questioned again. Is that clear?"

While Kate laid down the new rules of the game to Peterbroome, her father had begun to stand straighter, the cringing, shrinking old man of the night before seemed to be fading. That, too, didn't last long.

Kate's eyes blazed. 'Don't threaten me ever, ever again."

"I will do as I please. Always have and always will," Peterbroome replied smugly, returning to the attack. "Women don't dictate to me. Ever."

"You may have met your match in me," Kate declared, not at all convinced that her bluff was true. "Overstep the line, John, and I will find a way to blacken your name so badly that no woman in society will have you, your grandfather notwithstanding."

Peterbroome smiled at her. She didn't like it. Was he changing his tactics? This frightened her more than his storms.

"I told you once, my grandfather doesn't rule my life," he said lazily. "If I choose not to marry you after all, but expose your father's crime and throw him to the mercy of every member of every club he belongs to, then what will you say? If he is the gentleman he purports to be, he will take a gun to his miserable head. He is a common coward and a common thief, and the world will see him for what he is when I am through with him."

"Please." Grovenor appealed to Kate.

"Do you want your father's ignominious death on your head, my dear?" Peterbroome crowed. "What will your chances of a brilliant marriage be then? Zero, I warrant."

Kate wanted to cover her ears and blot the two poor excuses for men out of her brain. Her rebellion, seemingly so close to success, was in collapse at her feet again. Ruining Peterbroome was one thing—a mercy for sure—but her father's death, which she knew was more than likely the way he would salve his conscience, was far different.

"Get out of my room," Kate screamed, but not before Peterbroome patted Grovenor's cheek in mock triumph.

"You and your daughter will behave exactly as I wish—won't you?"

Kate watched Peterbroome leave, his manner jaunty and triumphant. She rose from her bed to bathe and dress. Charlie would be waiting for her. She needed him as never before.

Chapter Twenty-two

Nick appeared early and waited at the appointed bench in Kensington Gardens before the usual summer society parade arrived. He was happily supplanting Charlie, who had been forced to break his date with Kate after a peremptory summons from his father.

Nick understood Charlie's reluctance to ask him to meet Kate. Hadn't he told him enough times how useless it was to continue to see Kate and to love someone who did not and could not love him in return? How inadequate words were. How he felt about Kate was more than any of the usual words could describe. Love. Desire. They were nothing more than hollow sounds.

Kate was the other side of him. Hopeless? Possibly. That she would never be his had been obvious from the start. Maybe he wouldn't die if he never saw Kate again, but life would be pale and empty. Time to face that terrible prospect would come soon enough. He had today. It was an unexpected gift.

He saw Kate long before she saw him, and that suited Nick to a tee. It wasn't often that he had the chance to study her like this. All other times they were hemmed in by masses of people, except the week in her morning room on the Australian report or the few hours when he showed her around Delacourt House, her eyes large with excitement, schemes and plans for decoration spilling over her like a cascade. Still he could hardly have had the courage to feast his eyes and study her as he could now.

Her superb walking dress of lavender silk and lace flowed about her tall, slender figure like so many dancing elves, and her stride was so graceful she put every woman he had ever seen to shame. Nick's lips went dry at the sight of Kate's costume clinging deliciously to her breasts, his nighttime dreams come to life in the sunshine.

Nick turned around to compose himself. It wouldn't do for Kate or the world to see how much he wanted her. The thought of Peterbroome having all of Kate to himself drove him nearly off his head whenever he imagined them together. He paced the area around the bench to keep from exploding. Soon, as calm as he could ever be in Kate's presence, he went to meet her.

Kate's maid hovered over her with a parasol, and fortunately Kate fended her off. Nick was grateful. Any covering would mar his view of her face, the perfection of classic English beauty, clear brow, skin like marble come alive, straight nose and curving mouth that could only have been chiseled by a master hand. Travail only made Kate, in his eyes at least, more beautiful than ever. He quickened his pace.

At first Kate thought it was Charlie, but her cousin's slight build didn't compare in the least with the height and breadth of the man walking toward her. It couldn't be Nick. He was still in the country, or was supposed to be. She had excellent long sight, and by narrowing her eyes, she saw who it was. She felt giddy. If her battered heart needed balm, and it did very much, the sight of her love was all she needed to feel the healing begin.

His tailor did him proud in a gray light coat and unmentionables, his linen, white as ocean foam; a large intaglio dangling from a thick gold chain across his vest, made him elegance personified. The fine white thorn cane she had insisted that he buy completed the picture of the born Corinthian. Kate imagined midnight eyes full of life and promise smiling a welcome. Kate waved to Nick and slowed her step. How often do I get the opportunity to stare at him with impunity? How long will it be before my marriage distances Nick Monroe from me forever?

The hell with it, Kate said to herself. The future will take care of itself. It is a wondrous day. I am young and strong and hopeful, and I will have Nick Monroe to myself for a while, and that is all that matters to me. She quickened her pace and smiled from her heart.

Kate's radiance drew Nick, and he abandoned all gloom for the moment and as long as the day lasted.

"You are a surprise. What has brought you back to London so soon?" Would he say he couldn't stand being without her? Nonsense, of course, but even her common sense wasn't going to spoil the unexpected treat.

"You brought me back," Nick said. Tell the truth and shame the devil.

Kate laughed, almost stumbling over her feet. He had just given her the sun out of the sky.

"Mother and I adored your latest drawings, and I left at once to set them in train," he lied.

Nick took back the sun. The idea is to love me *and* my designs, a voice roared in Kate's head.

"Do I get to help you shop?" Kate chose to take whatever she could get of Nick. "I shall clear everything for the next three days."

Nick was delighted. Any terms under which he had Kate to himself were acceptable. His little white lie about the reason he returned to London, while only half true, would do. In actuality, he had returned to beard Maitland and Brown and settle some matters with Hooper. He had need of a great deal of money. Nick understood he was chasing rainbows trying to assist Kate out of her marriage, but he was not one to give up easily. And now that he had seen Peterbroome at his worst, a deadly loser, Nick's mission was fast becoming a crusade.

"Where do we start our shopping?" Kate asked merrily.

"I must find someone who can sell me a herd of red deer and some especially elegant pheasants," Nick said smiling, hoping she wouldn't laugh at him.

"You mean to emulate Castle Howard?"

"I want Delacourt House to be as memorable as I can make it, but I don't want to be ridiculous," he said sheepishly. "Do you think I will?"

Kate couldn't imagine Nick ever being outré. Charlie

was right. His mentor might have had hard beginnings, but between Mrs. Monroe, who seemed a formidable woman of fine breeding, and Nick's own innate taste, he had far exceeded her cousin's tutelage or any assistance of hers.

"I am in great need of carpets, small pieces of furniture, and masses of chintzes."

"If Ackermann's is good enough for the Regent's bedroom at Carlton House, will they do for you?" she asked.

"I think so." Nick laughed. He was feeling on top of the world. He would have Kate to himself for a few days. What more could he ask?

Kate took Nick's arm, and they spent the next hour-and-a-half talking amiably about wall hangings, pictures, dishes, and everything but what really mattered to them both. Kate was alternatively gay and pensive, chiding and sympathetic, and he adored her in each change of mood.

A light rain surprised them, and he hurried Kate into an ornamental gazebo, unwilling to release the feel of her hand on his arm. He wanted to remove her glove and bring her hand to his lips. It would not be enough to satisfy his longing to have all of her in his hands, his mouth over every inch of her body, to feel her at one with him. Unwillingly, Nick stopped his wayward longings as soon as they threatened to break their bounds.

Thunder and lightning crackled; the rain poured.

Kate waited. Was she wrong? Was Nick actually looking at her with love? She was so unsure. She had to know. She moved close to him.

Nick stepped back. He was afraid she would come too close, and he would be lost.

"It is only a summer rain, Lady Kate," he said, his voice a croak in her ears. "Nothing to worry about."

"Of course." Kate's breath was ragged, and she tried to laugh. It was her actress way of suppressing tears of loss and disillusionment. She moved to the edge of the shelter.

"I must hurry. Good-bye, Mr. Monroe, My father and Lord Peterbroome wish to dine early before the opera."

Nick's heart fell. For a precious few moments he had forgotten the real world. Of course, her fiancé must always have first claim on her, aided and abetted by her father. They and society were his enemies.

"May I see you home?"

"No, thank you. I rather like walking in the rain."

Nick started to insist, but Kate's eyes, now devoid of all feeling, had closed down. He felt shut out as surely as if she had closed a door in his face.

"Do you have a message for Charlie?" Nick asked, anything to keep Kate by his side a second longer. "He thought you might have tremendous news for him."

This time Kate looked at Nick directly, and he was sure she didn't see him.'

"It doesn't matter anymore," she said listlessly. "For a few hours I thought I'd regained mastery of my life. I haven't. You might tell him that."

Before Nick could ask for an explanation, Kate was gone, setting a rapid pace.

Kate was in a brutal tear. What was it that they called her, the Charmer? What a laugh. What a rotten joke. She had very nearly thrown herself into Nick's arms and was rebuffed in no uncertain terms for her presumption. Though what she knew about depressing the hopes and dreams of someone in love would fill the Thames and then some. Is that what I did to the men who had danced attendance on me for years, take their affection and hope of heaven away from them by failing to give them any part of me? A kiss? A simple, harmless embrace? Poor, poor darlings. Now that I know what it is to crave love and to be spurned, I apologize with all my soul. I served you ill.

Kate felt tears running down her face, wiped them savagely away with her gloves, and took the steps on her house on a run.

"Jenkins, is my father at home?" she asked the butler.

He nodded toward the library.

Pearson Grovenor was in almost the same state of gloom in the same chair as the night before.

Kate took a long drink from the heavily etched balloon glass at his elbow. Her father stared in disbelief.

"Do not fret, sir, the marriage to save your name is safe."

Chapter Twenty-three

Days later, Nick was still thinking about the day at the park.

If Kate was inconsolable, Nick was numb with misery. If Kate thought she was innocent about desire, Nick was certain he knew nothing about love or women.

Women played only the smallest part in Nick Monroe's life before Kate. He had seen too much of the anguish and destruction of men's lives from a few hours in a dockside brothel or a few stolen moments in a prostitute's arms in a doorway. He wanted none of that for himself. For several years he kept a Chinese courtesan in the Orient and an American widow in the Northwest. There had never been talk of love or anything permanent, and that was what he thought he wanted. But they weren't the enchanting Kate. Hardly Kate.

Nick relived every moment of the afternoon in the park for hours on end. He was no nearer understanding the complex emotions he sensed running between them before her departure than when it happened. He couldn't fathom why she seemed distraught when she left him. He had tried to be discretion itself. Hadn't he reined himself in like a galloping stallion? It was an unfortunate image, he told himself, but it was the truth. Had he given himself away again without realizing it? He groaned. It might indeed explain her sudden flight, so like the afternoon at Tattersall's. He must watch himself. He must not burden Kate with knowledge of a love she did not want or could not return.

At times Kate seemed fond of him, but the least overture

toward her seemed to frighten her away. He was at a terrible standstill.

Their subsequent shopping expeditions were hurried, all business and all too brief. Nick felt her constraint and that left him empty and sore at heart. If only he were clever enough to extricate Kate from Peterbroome. It was wishing on a star, he knew, but he would never give up trying until she was well and truly Peterbroome's bride.

Charlie found him lying full length on the couch in the Audley Street house, the Monroes' temporary home. Nick had begged off all social engagements for a week, and Charlie was there in answer to a note Nick had sent him that afternoon.

"It's only a few days, I know, but have you found out what Kate meant in the message she had me give you the other day?"

"Not really. She is very subdued these days."

Slayton eyed the drinks table across the room. It wasn't often he wanted the dubious consolation of liquor, but he did whenever life got too complicated, as it was at the moment. Keeping sober was a constant battle, but he was winning. This was one of those battles.

"Kate appears to have finally accepted marrying Peterbroome," Charlie said, studying Nick's face closely. "She has society on its ear for refusing all prenuptial entertainments, but she and Peterbroome are seen and promised everywhere."

"Do they seem affectionate toward each other?" Nick bit his lip.

"Peterbroome seems quite attached to her." Charlie knew he was putting a nail in Nick's dreams, but it was useless to lie. He would see for himself once he resurfaced.

"And what of Kate?" Nick asked cautiously.

"She is the same. Always Kate. A little more remote; her wit sharper than ever. If she is still against the marriage, she has become passive at least. She's a great actress, you know."

Nick's legs came off the couch in a high arc. Did Charlie know anything about his cousin's other life? He had always thought only he and Barkley of her world knew anything. He watched Charlie carefully. He had to know the truth, and rummaged in his mind for a way to settle the matter.

"How dare you call Kate an actress?" he said, moving to the fireplace.

"Turn of phrase, old boy," Charlie said easily.

Nick was satisfied for the moment. But Charlie was far more perceptive than most people credited him. It was imperative that they move on to talk of other things quickly. The last thing Nick wanted was to compromise Kate's secret life.

"I am bored to tears. What's on for the rest of the week?" Nick asked soon after.

"We have a mill about twenty-five miles from Windsor on Friday, but we must be back on the Saturday for the Duchess of Gloucester's party."

Nick wailed.

"Ungrateful lout," Slayton said, throwing a newspaper at his head. Nick caught it and laughed.

"How long since you would have given your last groat for an invitation to a royal do?" Charlie said rudely. "And this, the biggest event of the season, dear idiot, will be something special. They say 1600 invitations were delivered for a house that holds 600."

"To be a bloody gadabout with a life in pursuit of pleasure was never what I wanted for myself," Nick protested. "When I saw how you lived at the Albany, I knew I, too, wanted to be surrounded by beautiful things and must learn all I could about art and furniture."

Nick paced the room.

"I never intended to enter society when I came to London, but after seeing Kate for the first time, I wanted entry to find her. All I knew was that she rode in a crested carriage and might be a grand lady or a courtesan. I wanted to see her again and get her out of my mind for once and all time."

A part of Charlie was pleased that he had long since guessed Nick's reasons for wanting to be a proper cavalier. The other part decried his and Kate's success with Nick.

From an uncomplicated, devil-may-care fellow, Nick had become broody and testy. And Kate the same. The two people most important to him were dismally unhappy, and he couldn't do a damn thing about it.

"What is on for tonight?" Nick asked. He needed relief from his own company, and wanted it as soon as possible. He'd waited uselessly to hear from Maitland about the Australian project. More important, he wanted confirmation of his belief that there was something sinister about Peterbroome's willingness to marry Kate, when she clearly loathed him. His head hurt from thinking so much and wanting the impossible.

"A cockfight, I hear, a new dancer at the opera, a new chef at Boodle's, and a grudge match over billiards at White's, between Carlisle and Ort-Haven," Charlie said, ticking off the evening's offerings.

"All of them," Nick said, sounding far more exuberant than he was.

Charlie was delighted, and they parted soon after to dress for the evening.

Nick saw Charlie out himself. He refused to call the old butler who came with the house and was too old for the steep steps from the servants' quarters below. If the old man agreed, Nick was going to offer him an easy retirement soon, probably at Delacourt House. He loved doing things for people, heritage from his days as a homeless, lonely wanderer, and Nick wanted his estate to be a haven for everyone he was responsible for. It was a dream he never shared with anyone, afraid he'd be thought a candidate for bedlam.

Walking up to his room, Nick decided to write a letter to Hooper. It looked as if Kate no longer needed his help or his money for exile to the relative at the back of beyond. All the colorful language he had learned all over the world came out in a virtuoso stream of blue oaths.

At the head of the stairs, Nick heard a pounding at the door. It was Barkley, and he was white-faced and furtive.

"I have news for you, gov," he said, his head swiveling to see if they were overheard.

Nick led him back to the library and gave him a drink.

"You asked me to keep an eye out for you," he said, taking a deep swallow. "Peterbroome knocked my master about a week ago, and her ladyship had her hands full keeping him from killing her father. The book room was a shambles. Me and the butler were the only ones allowed in the room to set it to rights."

"Did he harm Lady Kate?"

"Not as I know, gov."

"Thank God for small mercies," Nick growled.

Nick realized that Peterbroome must have transferred his anger against Maitland to Grovenor and followed him home. Using the older man as an easier target to avenge his wounded pride was exactly what Nick would expect from someone of Peterbroome's stripe.

Why didn't Kate tell me about Peterbroome's beating her father when we met in the gardens? The answer was clear. She had come to tell Charlie about the beating, and, seeing him instead, put on a performance of nonchalance, probably the best acting role of her life. To make the whole affair even stranger—Kate hadn't told Charlie, or he would surely have told him at once. Everyone knew Charlie could never keep a secret.

Nick tried to decide whether he wanted to strangle or kiss Kate. He'd always known she was not one to wear her heart on her sleeve, and that would explain her peculiar behavior at Kensington.

Nick began to be concerned that Kate might be Peterbroome's next victim, and weighed what he could do to safeguard Kate in the future. Clearly, Peterbroome was capable of anything.

Barkley finished his drink, and Nick refilled it.

"I heard Jenkins tell his wife the master did something terrible, but he didn't know what, and that's why her ladyship has to marry Lord John."

Nick grabbed Barkley by the collar.

"If the butler heard that, he heard more," Nick said. "Find out what it is, and I'll set you up for life."

"I tried, gov," he said, as Nick let him go. "Jenkins is a

clam. Never gossips. Only reason he said what he did was that wife of his was plaguing him. The other servants are scandalized by the goings-on, and want to seek employment elsewhere."

It was useless to hound Barkley further. He would have to be content for the moment with knowing that he and Slayton were right about the betrothal having a sinister side.

Nick had no intention of waiting for Barkley to get the rest of the story out of Kate's butler. Who was to say that Peterbroome would confine his foul temper to Kate's father? If he touched her, Nick would make sure that Peterbroome never hurt anyone again. Kate might not love him, but his love for her, though hopeless, was beyond anything he had ever expected to feel for any woman. He could not hope to marry her, but he saw himself as the guardian of her happiness. His love was such that he knew he could not rest until she found someone who could make her happy. There were hordes of admirers waiting for Kate to beckon them, but the trick was detaching Peterbroome from her life. A tall order indeed. It was a terrible tangle.

Nick turned his attention to Barkley to continue his watch over Kate, and sped up the stairs. Charlie didn't know it yet, but they were going to have a different program than planned for the evening.

Chapter Twenty-four

Nick and Charlie stood at the back of Covent Garden, the music and the dancing of less than passing pleasure. The two had haunted the usual clubs before dinner, and left word everywhere for Tarn Maitland and Nevil Browning. The couples were inseparable. As a last resort, they visited Captain Black and White's house. The Maitlands' legendary Nanny Parker called down from the top of the stairs the suggestion that the family was expected at the opera house.

Leaving Manchester Square, Charlie stood stock-still. "I am starving, old man, and this can surely wait until tomorrow."

Nick turned on Charlie and showed such a face of agitation that Slayton reared back in alarm.

"Is it Kate again?" he asked softly. "I want only what is good and right for you. If she has accepted her fate, you must honor her decision. She will make the best of her marriage. Better women have endured worse. In time she will make a life apart from Peterbroome. I told you society treads a road of its own."

Charlie was right, of course. He has warned me and suffered with me over my obsession, but all the arguments in the world will not dissuade me until I know why my Kate must marry Peterbroome.

"I will accept everything when I am damn sure Kate isn't a hostage and is no longer coerced."

Charlie shook his head.

"Stop fooling yourself, Nick. You just told me she rebuffed you at Kensington. What do you need, a picture? Can't you take no for an answer?"

"No."

Charlie threw up his hands and they mounted the stairs of the opera house in uncomfortable silence, Nick at his heels.

When they finally spotted Tarn deeply enthralled in the dancing of La Angiolini, Nick was at first relieved and then struck dumb. Had he placed mythical powers in a man he hardly knew because he was selfish and desperate to have Kate for his own? Perhaps Charlie was right, and he was not helping Kate at all.

Nick knew his stubbornness against all odds had gotten him away from the penury of Australia, but was it now making him chase rainbows? He couldn't shake the facts, no matter how he tried to hide them. Kate had not told him or Charlie about the beating. She must have been ashamed, too proud to cry on a willing shoulder. Had he the right to divulge that shame to Maitland as well as Slayton? He was no longer as sure as he had been when he left Audley Street. That was the trouble He wasn't sure about many things lately.

"I don't want to bother Maitland and spoil his evening," Nick whispered to Charlie standing next to him. "I will have a note taken to his house, and offer to meet him at any time or place of his choosing."

"We are here. Let's get whatever is gnawing at you out in the open," Charlie offered, making his way toward the stairs soon after the performance drew to a clamorous finale.

"No," Monroe called out, pulling him back. "We will do it my way. All I ever do is ask the poor man to do me favors."

Charlie turned back. "Are you afraid that Tarn will not see you?"

Nick nodded. It was just as well that Charlie had it wrong. It meant fewer explanations. They turned, leaving the theater, when Tarn came up behind and tapped Nick on the shoulder. Without question, Charlie joined the others trailing in Maitland's wake.

"I'd like a word with you." Maitland proceeded to set a long pace.

"Your Australian proposals have been turned down by the government out of hand," Maitland said. "I am deeply sorry. You made a good argument for relief of the situation, but they say they have heard all the charges before."

"I am more grateful for your efforts than I can say, Captain," Nick said, offering his hand. Maitland took it.

"As to the matter of my Lord Peterbroome and Lady Katherine, I have only little to tell you."

Nick stopped.

"Some of my men have learned that Kate's father was caught cheating at cards, and is convinced Peterbroome stands between him and disgrace," Maitland said.

"You *are* the miracle worker everyone said you are," Nick said feelingly.

"Don't believe everything you hear, Monroe," Tarn cautioned. "You and Kate are no better off than before. You and I may have reasons to hate Peterbroome, but he is a canny bastard with very powerful friends. I am sorry I can't help you both."

Nick would not be dissuaded from seeing a light in the darkness, and said so.

"Kate is a glorious girl, and Lady Barbara and I want only the best for her. But she has turned down good men," Tarn said, with care. "Don't break your heart. There is just so far the people who run this country will allow people like you and me into their inner circle, and that particularly means marrying their women."

"If I may be so bold, sir. I am told Lady Barbara and you were in the same position once."

"I, Mr. Monroe, was extraordinarily lucky. My wife didn't give a tinker's damn about society, and I shared that feeling with her. We still do."

Nick understood.

Maitland offered his hand. Nick took it, then watched the big, lithe, athletic figure walk toward his carriage, where his wife, the Brownings, and Charlie awaited him. What an extraordinarily kind man, Nick thought, and waited for Charlie to rejoin him.

Kate was leaving the opera house at the same moment, walking unsmilingly between her father and fiancé. She turned and saw her friends gathered in a group. To Nick, standing apart, the sight of her was everything. He lifted his silk hat and saluted.

All the grief Kate had endured during the performance was suddenly worth it: Peterbroome playing the fond lover to the hilt for the benefit of his friends, her father urging her to act the simpering fiancée.

It was all unendurable, until she spied Nick at the rear of the stalls. She could see the clean, taut lines of his face, and the traces of suntan still remaining from the long voyage to England. She was memorizing the crisp hair, the color of port. Kate had an irresistible urge to rumple Nick's hair, her fingers deep in the thick curls. It was a thrilling wish, one she had never had before. Each encounter opened new vistas of man and woman pleasures that were breathtaking and vivid beyond her experience or imagination.

Peterbroome discovered she was watching Nick.

"I will not have you making a fool of me with these ceaseless attentions to that yokel," John Peterbroome told her. "Whether you like it or not, you are mine. The whole world knows it, even if you don't."

Kate turned wildly around to stare Peterbroome down.

"You don't own me now or ever," she said, her voice bordering on a scream. "You may have my father tamed, but not me. Leave me in peace."

"Not a hope," he said, laughing as if she had just made a famous joke. "I'll run that lout through if I see him within a yard of you. And any other man will suffer the same fate."

Kate was appalled and rose to stalk out of the box. Peterbroome put his hand on her arm with such force that a pain shot like liquid heat up to her shoulder, and she cried out.

Around them people made impatient noises, and she and

Peterbroome remained separated in anger until the end of the performance.

And now, here was Nick, so close and yet so far away. And that was the way it would always be. Peterbroome was capable of anything, and Kate feared his twisted mind had seized on Nick for no discernible reason other than his crazed, twisted possessiveness. She knew for certain Peterbroome would never be content until he avenged himself on Nick or Charlie. She needed to tread carefully from now on. She started at once.

Kate smiled and waved to everyone, except Nick, and abruptly turned toward her father's carriage.

She would write to them tonight and beg them to stay away. If Peterbroome made good his threat, what little was left for her to live for would be destroyed in one strike.

Lord John Peterbroome had her and her father right where he wanted them. Spiders caught in his web.

Chapter Twenty-five

Charlie dismissed his coachman, and he and Nick left Covent Garden and walked home. It was not the smartest thing to wander aimlessly in certain parts of London, but they felt quite able to handle themselves. The few toughs and rough-looking men they encountered on their ramble gave them a wide berth. They might take on one drunken toff, but two sober dandies as big and virile as Nick and Charlie might not be such easy prey.

They were right. Nick's cane concealed a lethal Toledo sword, and inside Charlie's coat was a small knife left over from his wild-boy days. After a while, Charlie stopped Nick in mid-stride.

"Are you going to tell me about your conversation with Tarn Maitland?" asked Slayton, no longer able to mask his curiosity. He had been left out of a discussion he was sure was important.

Nick shrugged and walked a few steps and came back. He took Charlie's arm and pulled him along.

"If what I tell you gets out," Nick warned, "I will throttle you. Kate's reputation is at stake."

Charlie pledged his discretion, and Nick told him word for word what he had learned from Maitland.

"I knew it had to be a shattering reason," Slayton shouted. "My grand-bloody-uncle a common, bloody cheat. What a pity I can't tell Papa. It would add ten years to his life."

Nick eyed Charlie speculatively. "Do you think Kate knows?"

"It would explain this sudden docility of hers," Charlie

conceded. "She appears to have accepted the marriage, and I can tell you without equivocation, keeping the family name from scandal would be paramount to the Grovenors, father and daughter."

Nick knew it, but had to hear it from Charlie.

"No wonder she was so distant with me and abbreviated your shopping," Charlie added. "She is ashamed, and there isn't anything we can do for her."

Nick felt violence building up in his brain. All his grandiose plans to rescue Kate were going up in smoke. He felt more powerless than ever in his life. Unless she gave him permission to free her, if he could find a way to free her, he and Charlie were at a complete standstill. Tarn had intimated that earlier in the evening.

"Do you believe Kate's father is a cheat?" Nick was still grasping at straws, exactly what Maitland had warned him against.

"I'd believe anything of that worm."

"Dishonesty? Scandal? Enough to ruin his reputation, ruin his daughter and the family name?"

Charlie walked in a fevered circle.

"Grovenors have always been family proud, and much as I want to believe he did it, I must admit I find it hard to think of him as a complete rogue."

Nick nodded.

"Was my uncle drunk when they played cards?" Charlie asked. "Did Peterbroome play in the game?"

"Yes, but Peterbroome was playing in another room," Nick answered. "I asked Maitland all these questions, too."

They were nearing the Albany, tired and depressed for Kate's future, and sorry for themselves.

Chapter Twenty-six

"The monster!" Charlie Slayton exploded when he finished reading a note from Kate over his breakfast the next morning.

Kate had begged him to stay away from her, and to bid Nick do the same.

"I am satisfied that P is quite out of his mind and capable of anything. I wish you and M to keep far away from me," Kate had written, "especially M. There is nothing you can do for me now. I am watched constantly."

Charlie threw the letter across the table. To show it to Nick would be courting disaster. He had to find a way to tell Nick without raising his temperature, and that was a tall order.

Not too far away, Nick was boiling. He had an insulting letter from Peterbroome ordering him to keep away from Kate. An accompanying note from her broke their last shopping appointment. It was curt, and left no doubt she wanted nothing to do with him ever again.

"Have you any idea what is in this note or what cause her ladyship could have to write to me, Barkley?" Kate's servant, who had delivered the letter, was standing just inside Nick's office in great agitation. It was a nonsensical question, and he knew it. But he was at his wit's end.

"I didn't see my mistress. I was asked by the new butler to deliver this and one to Lord Charles," the hulking giant said. "But I can tell you there's all hell let loose at the house."

Nick didn't like the sound of it.

"That man, Peterbroome, is replacing all the indoor servants with his own people," he said, becoming red in the face. "I was told Lady Kate is distressed, and her father goes to bed with a bottle and rarely leaves the house."

"What about your position?"

"I am safe for the moment," Barkley said. "I'm handy around the house and the stables. No one knows my special place with Lady Katherine."

Nick rose and came to stand in front of Barkley.

"You'll always have a place with me, but try to stay at the house as long as you can," Nick said, putting an arm across Barkley's shoulders. "I still need to know if your mistress is in physical danger and needs my protection."

Nick rang for the butler, who arrived with Matt Meredith, the estate manager, in a lather of gloom. Barkley left without a word.

"What are you doing here, Matt?" Nick asked.

"Your mother sent me, sir," the old man replied bleakly. "I'm to bring you home as quick as may be, she said."

That didn't sound like his mother, and Nick was instantly alarmed.

"What's happened? Is she ill? Tell me, man!"

"My orders are to see you and bring you home. That's all I will say."

Nick didn't understand. It was so unlike his mother to admit she needed anyone, and he made haste to leave.

Before Kate came into his life, his mother was the most important person in his world, the impetus for all of his ambitions. Within half an hour Nick was out of the house, poor old, grizzled Matt Meredith panting behind him. It was early morning, and Nick drove like a charioteer in ancient Rome, making only a short stop at the Albany to inform Charlie where he was going and to ask him to watch over Kate for him.

"Now tell me once again, slowly, what happened?" Nick asked Matt as they approached the London suburbs.

"Mrs. Monroe was rummaging through the house again, as she's been doing since the moment you left, sir," the older man explained. "Your mother, if you don't mind my saying so, is not one to seek help or let a servant do anything she thinks she can do better."

Nick understood. His mother was almost too fiercely independent at times and from the beginning fought all his efforts to give her everything he thought a woman could want—dresses, homes, jewels. Vivian Monroe resisted him at every turn until Nick wore her down, and she accepted a modest house and one servant, but few other luxuries. Indeed, his mother opposed his raging appetite for money when he was young, and only his fortuitous kidnapping by the mate got him away from her and Australia. Moving to England was another struggle, but as always, Nick conceded, his will more than equaled hers at the end of the day.

Whatever was wrong with his mother was his fault. He should have been there to help her adjust to living in the house and not have left so soon after Kate's visit. Was his helpless addiction for Kate ruining his judgment? He would have to think about that at length, but not now. Time enough after he got to Delacourt House and learned what was troubling his mother.

Nick turned to the old man beside him.

"So she worked herself into a frenzy?"

"She was exhausted, sir, but I don't think it was that," Meredith said nervously. "Your mother had a visitor. He stayed a very long time."

"Who was it?"

"He wouldn't give his name, just demanded to be taken to the mistress, and then ordered the servants to leave."

Nick stiffened. "My mother permitted this?"

"He whispered something to her, and she sent everyone off."

"And?"

"When the man left, your mother collapsed."

Nick felt a glacial cold take hold, and he let the horses have their heads as soon as they hit open country, too upset to revel in the speed and endurance of the grays as promised by the man at Tattersall's.

Hours later he spied the large and fashionable hostelry he had used on his first journey down to Delacourt, and pulled in for a change of horses. Nick managed a bun and a cup of tea, paid the landlord handsomely to have the best hack made available at once, and was off and away in moments, leaving Meredith to follow with a phaeton and a fresh team of horses.

Nick arrived at the estate and was in his mother's room a few moments later. Matters were even worse than he imagined. Vivian Monroe was a wraith and seemed to have aged terribly since he last saw her. Tears ran in rivulets down her weathered face, her eyes haunted, unlike anything he'd seen in the worst days of their early life in Australia.

Nick ran to the bed and gathered her in his arms. She struggled and pushed him away, and Nick was flabbergasted. Never in all these years together had she ever behaved this way toward him.

"Mam, what is it? Tell me," Nick pleaded.

"Your father was a thief."

Chapter Twenty-seven

Nick reared back as if she struck him.

"He wasn't duped by Guy and the Delacourts after all," Mrs. Monroe spat out. "He knew exactly what he was doing when he aided and abetted Guy Delacourt in robbing and stealing from his friends' homes. They hid the evil things in an abandoned house near here ready for crooked London dealers sent by your father to collect in the dead of night."

Nick tried to shut his ears. He couldn't bear having his faith in his father shattered.

"He made fools of us," she cried out, pounding the counterpane. "He destroyed our lives. He was a liar, and I should have known. I should have guessed."

Nick wandered aimlessly around the room. He had pitied Kate for having a father lost to all decency. Clearly they shared fathers who would forfeit their children's rightful heritage without a second thought. It was another bond they had, but one that would, now more than ever, keep them apart.

"Say something, Nick," his mother pleaded.

"How could he have duped us all those years?"

"He always laughed about my principles. I never knew that he was laughing at *me*. More stupid, lovesick fool I. Remember that, Nick, love kills, and you know it from my experience, if nowhere else."

All Nick's life Vivian Monroe had imposed her own impossible standards of honesty on him, citing his father as a model of virtue. Nick could imagine her outrage at learning that her ideal, the taproot of her existence, had deceived her into following him to Australia to live a life of desperate poverty and isolation.

Nick felt the same searing disappointment that the man he knew only as a bluff, devil-may-care father, transported unfairly to Australia, was, in fact, guilty of the charges laid against him. True, he had seen more of the world than his mother, and he knew dishonesty was a way of life for many people. It was not his way, and never would be. He'd had probity drilled into him from childhood, and he believed in all the rules his mother had taught him. In point of fact, his scrupulous honesty had gained him the absolute trust of the American captain he rescued. Later all his business dealings, including those with the Chinese, were based on a handshake. He would have it no other way.

Yet he found it impossible to believe he and his mother could have been so wrong for so long.

"Mam, are you sure about Papa?" Nick never had the nerve, even when he'd grown tall and rich, to question anything Vivian told him. He knew her well. Wonderful as she was, her years as a governess and making a life for them in the rough-and-ready ways of Australia had made her strong. Later, she had become unashamedly domineering and convinced of the rightness of her own way in everything. It had always been a joke between them. She was never wrong.

His mother left her bed, shouting and cursing, pulling at her hair and her clothes, her rage biblical. Nick had never imagined he would see his mother reduced to the wild woman descending on him now. He reached out for her, but she eluded him.

"You dare ask me if I can be wrong?" she growled, circling the room. Her grief was more terrible than anything Nick had ever seen. He was rooted to the floor in shock and grief.

"Would I blacken the name of the man for whom I gave up everything gladly, sacrificed your life, if I had had a scintilla of doubt about his innocence?" she screamed. "He swore on your head he was not guilty of any of the charges, and I believed him. It was always Guy Delacourt or his valet, Tom Travers, who had arranged the robberies and together blamed your father," Mrs. Monroe shouted. "He swore on your head he was innocent, but I should have known. Only your father had the brains among the three of them."

His mother was throwing around names from the dim past, names that had shadowed his childhood nightmares. He'd grown up believing that Winters, his father's employer, had convinced him to take the blame for Guy Delacourt's waywardness. In return, his father would be cleared of the charges and the family given enough money to live like lords in Canada.

"Then what is the truth?" Nick asked.

"It was your father who planned the robberies, saw to the sale of the plunder to London villains, and then cheated Guy and Tom out of their share," she said, the fires of rage only now beginning to abate. "Of course, Winters threw your father to the dogs. He never intended to help us once your father confessed his part and he got Guy Delacourt safely away to America."

Nick nodded dumbly.

"Where did the money come from that paid our passage to Australia," Nick asked, "from my father's robberies?"

"Yes. Your father told Travers where the money was. In the end, he had to give Tom his share." Mrs. Monroe returned to her bed.

"Where did you get this cock-and-bull story?" Nick asked, hoping against hope there was a hole somewhere in the sordid tale.

"Tom Travers told me everything," she said.

Nick whirled around.

"And you believe the word of that confessed thief?" Nick shouted.

Even as he said it, Nick knew by the utter defeat in her eyes that Tom Travers had told her the whole, searing truth.

After years of believing in his father's innocence, he had to begin thinking himself the son of a real criminal. The pain of truth took his breath away.

It was time to reexamine his life.

Chapter Twenty-eight

Kate sat cold as stone before the mirror, her maid in the last stages of dressing her hair and arranging the emeralds Peterbroome's grandfather sent down especially for the Gloucester party. The intricate antique silver mountings and green stones were heavy and cold on her throat. Kate couldn't help feeling they were more like a noose than a necklace encircling her throat.

Impatient to be gone, she bade the maid to hurry and help her into the shimmering pale green and silver dress that Peterbroome himself had chosen for her to wear.

If Kate had thought her many declarations of independence from the father and fiancé would prevail, she was wrong. Peterbroome treated Grovenor House as an extension of his own. She had ordered him to stay out of her sitting room, but to no avail. He was driving the new maid and housekeeper and others hired to replace her old retainers around the bend. When Kate refused point-blank to take part in selecting a gown to go with the jewelry, he took over the task. Every dress she owned had been paraded for him before he finally picked the one she was wearing.

For twopence she would have ripped off the jewelry and cried off, but the prospect of seeing Nick and Charlie was overriding. She knew her door was barred to all people Peterbroome didn't like, including the Maitlands and Brownings. Her protests had fallen on deaf ears, and Kate was beside herself, feeling caged and isolated.

Now bedecked and bejeweled, there was nothing left to delay her departure. She was forced to bow to Peterbroome's every wish and appear at his side happy and serene at a party that the *ton* was calling the crush of the season. Word was that hordes of society left town rather than admit they were not invited to the Gloucesters'. Yet Kate would gladly have given her invitation to those half-willing to mortgage their souls to be among the cream of society tonight.

Gathering her voluminous skirts around her, Kate descended the stairs and floated past her father and Peterbroome into the carriage. Marie Antoinette could not have felt more desolate in the tumbrel taking her to the guillotine.

Nick had a light dinner with his mother at ten o'clock. He had persuaded her to travel to London with him and now saw her comfortably settled in the largest bedroom in the London house, before running down the stairs into the street.

He was to meet Charlie at the party, and decided to walk. It was one of those unparalleled London midsummer nights, clear and dazzling with life and promise of pleasurable entertainments that once spoke volumes to Nick. Then London was the center of the longings that drove his youthful ambition for riches. Later London had magical powers for him because it was here he had met his Kate, his one and only love.

Tonight London was ashes for him. In the mood he was in, the night was ordinary. His father's guilt had made him question everything. Maybe his mother was right. England was no longer home. And now, without the remotest chance of having Kate as his wife, what did England, or any place for that matter, hold for him?

Nick shook his head trying to clear it of everything but the evening ahead, and he hurried on to meet Charlie. He didn't want to think about anything but seeing Kate. Charlie confirmed to him as soon as he returned to London that Kate was a virtual prisoner in her own home. She was seen day or night with her father or John Peterbroome, and at parties they never let her out of sight. It was becoming the talk of London.

His blood boiled, and he searched for ways to extricate her, knowing that nothing short of killing her father and Peterbroome would do. Nick had killed a man in China who attacked him with a knife, and had agonized over it for years. To kill in cold blood was beyond him, and he knew it. He rubbed the spot in his left shoulder where the knife had struck and was a constant reminder of a night he didn't like to think about.

He took a shortcut and arrived at a bedlam in the making before the towering Gloucester mansion.

Nick was struck, as always, by the teeming sense of life and the air of expectancy that surrounded all such occasions. An endless stream of wonderful carriages, each with lamps winking in the darkness, gathered from all sides of the converging roads near Hyde Park. Torches lit the outside of the imposing house. The clatter of horses on the cobbled stones was like the sound of a waterfall. Long, wide windows on every floor were opened to the air and glowed with hundreds of candles in chandeliers, giving many gawkers a glimpse of the fashionable milling inside. The music of roving violins and orchestras caught on the light summer breeze and floated cloudlike over commoner and aristocrat below.

Nick's height enabled him to see more than most of the gaping throng. Among the first was the Duke of Wellington, shorter than he expected, his often caricatured hook nose making it easy for Nick and the crowds to identify him. A cheer went up. Next came three Lord Mayors in full regalia, Lady Tavistock, and Lady Shelley, all of whom Nick had met in the weeks before the party.

Of all the balls and parties to which Charlie and Kate had taken him, none seemed as splendid as this. Nick had never seen so many powdered, gold-laced footmen, as tall as he, lining the steps at the entrance.

All at once Nick was rewarded. The Grovenor landau arrived, and Kate turned, saw him, and half waved. Peterbroome swiveled around, seemingly intent on finding who attracted her special attention. He took her arm possessively and hurried Kate up the mansion stairs. Nick turned

abruptly. Perhaps Peterbroome had not seen him. Nick
didn't want to add to her suffering.

He must be discretion itself from now on where Kate
was concerned, and the idea of it sent him into a frenzy.

"You look ready to commit mayhem, old boy," Charlie
said, approaching him on the left. Actually, Slayton had
been watching Nick from afar, and didn't like what he saw.
From the first he had been impressed by the handsome
Australian's open countenance, but even more by an optimism that was positively catching. But lately, it seemed to
Charlie, much of Nick's buoyancy had been erased, and all
because of Nick's feverish passion for his cousin. Or had
something new been added? That afternoon when they met
briefly, his friend looked hollow-eyed and listless. When
Charlie questioned Nick about the reason he'd torn down to
the country, Nick had been almost rude. Charlie knew he'd
hit on something, but this was not the time for probing into
mysteries.

"I'm for the festivities," Charlie said, walking beside
Nick toward the house.

The scene within the high-ceilinged, magnificently proportioned rooms was unbelievable. Guests were jammed to
the walls, an army of satin-clad and white-wigged servants
struggled to keep trays of liquid refreshments upright, and
not always successfully.

"Her Grace must be ecstatic," Charlie tried to say above
the crashing sound of voices and the music. "The house is
being shaken to its foundations."

Nick agreed, and together they struggled out of the first
room in search of quiet. They were separated by a crowd
gathered around the door, not to reunite for more than an
hour. That didn't bother Nick overmuch. He had come to
the party for only one reason, to see Kate and learn for himself if all that Barkley and Charlie had said about her im-
prisonment was true.

From time to time he saw Peterbroome with Kate, and
was careful to keep himself hidden. Considering he and
Peterbroome stood head and shoulders above most of the
others, it was not an easy task. What Nick wanted was the

chance to see Kate alone, separated from what he was calling in his mind her captor. A few minutes alone with Kate
was all he needed to assure himself of the state she was in.
This cat-and-mouse game was not to his liking, and his patience was fast beginning to wear thin. A half hour later
Charlie jostled him.

"I just heard our friend Peterbroome tell my uncle to
keep an eye on Kate," Charlie said, as if reading Nick's
mind. "He was invited to the card tables, and he can never
resist the lure of the counters. I was that way once."

He laughed and together he and Nick combed the rooms
as best they could, becoming separated once again. Nick
found Kate at last in one of the supper rooms. He wove between the hordes attacking the supper tables like a herd of
cows, and he came up behind her.

"Tell me what I am supposed to eat." Nick tried to be
offhand, when all he wanted was to touch her, to hold her.
"It looks like the duchess ransacked the whole of the world
for us."

Kate couldn't catch her breath. She had seen him a half-
dozen times, while Peterbroome held her arm in a grip of
steel all evening, and prayed Nick would not come near
her. Now he was close enough for her to smell his cologne,
feel his breath on her neck. She tried for a lightness, hoping
to fool Nick as well as herself and everyone pressing close
to them in the room.

"If you are very hungry, there are Perigord pies, truffles
from France, sauces and curry powders from India, ham
from Westphalia, reindeer tongues from Lapland," Kate re-
cited. His nearness sent her heart into a spin, her body vi-
brating like the strings of a Stradivarius. So much for
lightness she told herself.

"Sounds like the Grand Tour. Tell me more." Nick's
voice betrayed his yearning to touch her. Or so he thought.
No, he hoped.

"You want too much."

"I want everything," Nick said softly, the iron control he
had placed on himself all these weeks suddenly nonexis-
tent.

Kate dared not turn around. She was afraid to be disappointed again, to assume he felt something for her, wanted what she wanted.

"There are cheeses from Italy, and olives from Spain," Kate went on, her voice shaking, afraid to trust what her senses told her was lovemaking and her head told her was party talk.

"Is it true that you are a prisoner in your own home?"

"Go away, please, Nick." The name slipped out.

Nick was almost undone. How long he had wanted to hear his name in that thrilling, caressing voice that moved him beyond any voice he had ever heard.

"I want to help you, dear Kate."

"You can't. No one can."

The hell with the proprieties Nick decided, and turned Kate toward him. He saw his own misery mirrored in her eyes, and, lost to everything, began to take her in his arms.

Kate came to him, heedless of the stares and murmurs beginning around them.

Then someone gripped Nick's arm and rushed him away from Kate and the supper table. Nick turned ready for murder to see Charlie and Kate's father. They were both fuming, and before Nick could protest, very nearly frog-marched him to the nearest door.

"How dare you?" Nick demanded.

"How dare you jeopardize my daughter's reputation?" Pearson Grovenor demanded, drunk, bloodshot eyes like daggers. "Real gentlemen remember their place."

Nick bridled, his fists doubled.

Charlie elbowed Grovenor aside and, taking Nick's arm, propelled him into a side room.

"What the hell are you thinking behaving like a lovesick puppy?" Charlie said, throwing up his hands. "Peterbroome has formed a jealous rage against you and is capable of anything, not to mention putting Kate in a compromising position."

"Good. Maybe he'll take care and treat Kate properly," Nick said, knowing it was a poor defense for the damage he may have already inflicted on Kate.

"One doesn't play silly buggers with a rakehell like Peterbroome." Charlie struck the table. "Use your head. He is dangerous."

"So am I," Nick snapped. "I am sick and tired of the bastard having it all his own way."

"Better men than you have tried teaching John Peterbroome a lesson, and lived to regret it," Charlie said, his anger real and fiery. "I didn't agree to help you get into society to see you maimed for life by that madman and ruining Kate's life even more."

"Someone has to think about Kate," Nick shouted. "No one else gives a damn."

Nick was right, and Charlie knew it. He sat down in a chair and put his head in his hands.

"I feel as powerless as you do, but what can we do?" Charlie moaned. Unlike Nick, he'd given up the fight.

"I'm sorry." Nick was at Charlie's side. "I didn't mean what I said. I know as well as you do there is nothing to be done. I just hate everyone and everything making Kate marry a man she detests."

Charlie looked at Nick. He hated the bargain he had made with Vivian Monroe, but all at once he felt impelled to accede to her greater wisdom. For among all the other reasons he knew against Nick's ever marrying Kate was the word that night from Kate's father that Peterbroome threatened to kill Nick if he didn't stay away from Kate.

"It is time you and I had a serious talk again about Kate." For all the bluster in his voice, Charlie wasn't sure he was doing the right thing. "However much we dislike it, Kate is going to marry Peterbroome. He is a jealous bastard and possessive as hell. So that even after Kate produces the heir he needs, he will keep her on a short rein. Unlike many unhappily married women in that state of affairs who take lovers like bonbons, our Kate will never be like that. There will never be a future for the two of you."

He was quoting Nick's mother verbatim. Charlie hoped she was happy, because he was miserable, and Nick was more unhappy than he had ever seen him.

Chapter Twenty-nine

Nick left Charlie in the Duchess of Gloucester's small pseudo-Roman garden room.

But where was he going? To depart without apologizing to Kate was unthinkable. To go home only reanimated all thoughts of his mother's still haunted eyes and his father's fall from the pedestal they both placed him on all those years.

Nick wandered the house now even more densely packed than when he and Charlie had left the supper rooms. Men and women he had met in his circuit of London society were anxious to speak to him, and others he scarcely knew still gave him a wide berth. He didn't imagine he looked very inviting in the mood he was in. Or had he, as Charlie and Pearson Grovenor charged, compromised Kate so publicly that people were already talking? It was a chilling thought, and a reminder of how small and incestuous London was.

How reckless could anyone be? he cursed himself. Kate had looked at him meltingly, or so he wanted to think, and he threw all respectability away, and probably gave Peterbroome further cause to restrict Kate's movements and hate his guts.

The very idea of his guilt made him wild with anxiety and drove him back to Charlie.

"I have a big mouth, haven't I?" Charlie said morosely.

"No. But I am so confused about so many things," Nick said, wanting to tell Charlie about his father, and knowing he wouldn't. One didn't tell a friend, however dear, everything he wanted to tell Slayton. How do you say, "Remem-

ber that man, my father, the one I said I idolized, was as innocent as the driven snow? He was, in fact, a conniving,
calculating crook, who brought us all down with him."

Charlie watched Nick's face contort with pain. "I think
you need a drink. The clubs will be deserted. Anyone who
is anyone is here or hiding in mortification. No one wants
to admit he has been omitted from the guest list."

Charlie led the way to the hall to find they were facing
sudden pandemonium. Clearly most of the guests had chosen to leave the ball at the same time and created a perilous
situation, crowding, bordering on a riot, not in the least
helped by wild rumors. Listening closely, they heard someone say there was talk of fire somewhere, but to them it
sounded wholly unlikely. There was no evidence of smoke
or the sounds of fire apparatus, but the sense of panic was
deepening.

Taller than most, Nick and Charlie managed to peer over
the banister of the splendid staircase to see and hear
screaming men and women crushed against the walls all the
way down the steps. People were lumped together at the
front door waiting for their carriages to be delivered to
them in a sudden driving rain. The palpable sense of panic
and desperation led the Duke of Wellington, caught
halfway down the stairs, to cry out in his battlefield voice,
"Be calm. There is not the slightest danger." But to no
avail.

Women fainted and were trampled underfoot by the
surging crush, men tore at each other, screams rose to a
frightening crescendo. It was a scene few would forget.

Nick looked wildly about for a sign of Kate, and spied
her on the floor below pinned against flamboyant, twenty-
foot draperies gaping at the top to reveal that she was actually standing in front of a window and probably didn't
realize that escape was a few feet away. Nick pointed this
out to Charlie, and then hiked himself onto the banister,
sliding down to the bottom. He pushed his way savagely
out of the house to get around to the side, trying to decide
where the window could be. Judging correctly, he lifted the
window and pushed away the draperies. With his arms

around her waist, he raised Kate off her feet and past everyone out into the little garden behind them. Others who had seen them escape followed suit. Nick led her farther into the dense foliage.

"I hope your fiancé won't object," Nick said, letting her drop to her feet onto the grass wet with dew. "He doesn't love me, I hear."

"I do," she said under her breath.

"Say that again."

Kate wrenched herself free; tears flooded her eyes. She wiped them roughly with the back of her hand, turning away. He took her arm and forced her to face him.

"How can you marry Peterbroome?"

"God knows I don't want to, but I have no choice in the matter," Kate said, tears overflowing unchecked down her face. "He has some power over my father, but I can't talk about it. There is nothing anyone can do, nothing. You'll only make it worse. Peterbroome will kill you. Go away."

Nick pulled her to him roughly, all reason suspended in the need to hold her and wipe away her tears. He kissed her with all the pent-up need of weeks, gently forcing open her mouth with his tongue, a hunger running rampant over his frenzied need. His hands roamed over her shoulders down to her bosom, his face soon hidden in their roundness. How he had dreamed of this, prayed for the chance to lose himself in his love.

Kate timidly met him kiss for kiss, yearning for yearning, an overwhelming voyage of discovery. She was home at last. The glacier that had been her heart burst into a million shards. She followed Nick's every move with wonder, demanding release she had never known existed. The poets were right, of course. Love was soaring over the moon.

Nick pulled away, leaving Kate rocking perilously over an abyss of his making.

"What am I doing? Nick whispered, his voice breaking as he realized the wreckage his lapse had created. "I have to think sensibly for both of us."

Nick left her and went looking for Charlie. With one

glance at Nick's face, pale and bitter, his hair and cravat in disarray, Charlie pushed Nick aside and went to find Kate.

"Go home. I'll see you later."

"You unmitigated bastards, " Charlie said later, when he returned to find Nick slumped in a chair.

"Where's Kate?"

"I found her father. He took her home."

"Thanks, Charlie."

"You are a cad, and I am mortally disappointed in you," Charlie said. He was grim and angry.

"You can't hate me any more than I hate myself," Nick said.

"Why the hell did you have to kiss her?" Charlie hammered. "Hasn't she enough grief without your adding to it?"

"I couldn't help myself," Nick said, carefully omitting to say that he thought Kate said she loved him. Or was that his imagination? Too much had happened to make him sure of anything.

"Isn't she unhappy and vulnerable as it is without your muddying the waters and making her hopeful?" Charlie could have cut out his tongue. Did he say too much?

Nick watched Charlie closely.

Nick struggled over to Charlie. "Are you saying Kate loves me?"

Charlie was sick of the whole business: Mrs. Monroe and the devil's own pact he'd made with her to keep Nick away from Kate; society's long arm of retribution against a man whose father was a convict, however unjustly sentenced; and Peterbroome and Grovenor, a pair of immoral monsters, whose dissolute lives were forcing Kate into a marriage that would more than likely destroy her. And what about me? How long must I sit idly by and see my own darling Kate desire another man? How much can I take?

"Yes, Nick, I am saying that Kate loves you. And what can you do about it now that you know? Does it make a damn bit of difference, except hurt more?"

Nick stared at Charlie, his heart playing tricks, his hands hanging like stone beside him.

"You, of all people, should know how much it hurts, Charlie," Nick said. "Listen to me, and listen carefully. Kate would hate me if she knew my father was as guilty as the courts found him. Guilty! Do you hear me?" Nick was white and shaking, beads of perspiration standing out on his face.

Seeing the havoc, Charlie felt as if he had been struck.

"I don't know what to say," Charlie whispered, not sure what words of consolation would help a man as proud as Nick in the circumstances.

"Peterbroome is a terrible man, but he was born a gentleman. Maybe in the end he will realize his good fortune to have Kate and change his ways."

Charlie groaned inwardly, doubting that would happen. It was no time for skepticism.

Chapter Thirty

For Kate, the week after the near disaster at the Gloucesters' ball was the most searing of her life.

Reliving Nick's rescue and the moments after in the garden tore at her from every side, awake or asleep. Why in God's name had she told him she loved him and then thrown herself into his arms? What was the man to do? He held her and comforted her as any kind friend and gentleman would. It was what she did next that must have given him a disgust of her. As Kate saw it, she had forced Nick to forget himself, and then his good manners prevailed and he saved the day for both of them by going to find Charlie.

Was I so inept that he thought me a tart? And wasn't I one? The man saves me from being trod on and maybe killed. Do I thank him demurely, as I should? No. I make unseemly advances to him again and ruin everything. In his kindness, did Nick expect a chaste thank you and a kiss? Of course. But what do I do? I behave like a wanton, a mare in heat, an animal in a cage.

So much for my vaunted innocence. And what about my frigidity? The first man I want desperately touches me, and I make a bloody fool of myself. Never again, Kate vowed, would any man stir the new ice cap that had taken permanent residence in her heart. I won't allow anyone to awaken the ashes again. I can't die twice, can I?

Kate went to the window of the small sewing room overlooking the mews. She loved the sounds of activity surrounding the care of the family horses and carriages. The little room had become her refuge over the past weeks. It was the one place the new butler knew she could be found when she wanted solitude. Kate suspected that Jenkins had taken the man into his confidence, and sensed that he looked after her without arousing Peterbroome's ire.

Kate rarely left the house during the day, and only ventured out at night to placate her father and Peterbroome, who demanded she be seen about the town with them. She was cold as ice to them and barely acknowledged their existence.

There was a gentle knock on the door, and Kate took her time answering. She had an idea why she was wanted. She had succeeded in refusing to see Peterbroome during the day. But on the fourth day he began issuing threats through her father which became more and more difficult to withstand.

She was right, her father was at the door.

"Please see Peterbroome," Grovenor pleaded. "I know his temper, and have seen him cut off his nose to spite his face a dozen times."

"He needs me as much as you need his silence."

"He doesn't need your intransigence. If you want your married life to be peaceful, learn to curb that razor tongue of yours," her father argued impatiently.

The door flew open.

"How wise of you, Grovenor," Peterbroome said lazily. He pointed a dirty finger at Kate's father and motioned him out of the room.

"You can't be alone with Kate," Grovenor protested weakly.

"Don't be a fool. I can and will do precisely what I like and where I like," Peterbroome said harshly, closing the door after the older man. He turned on Kate.

"As for you, take your father's advice, my Lady Kate. I am implacable when thwarted, and you are fast becoming a thorn in my side. I will no longer tolerate it."

Kate spun on her heel and faced the window. Down below she saw Barkley in heated conversation with Nick Monroe. It was a strange sight. Peterbroome stole up behind her and saw what took Kate's attention, and exploded.

"I'm going to teach you a lesson you'd better not forget,"

he shouted. "You are mine, and don't forget it, now or ever. I will not have a profligate wife. You will know no other man but me for the rest of your life."

Peterbroome became more and more incensed, and suddenly another look, one Kate could only imagine as utter jealousy or mania, took over.

"I have ordered that lout away for the last time," Peterbroome cried, and went to the door. Opening it, he looked back, and seeing the fear in Kate's eyes, shut the door and covered the small space between them in a bound.

Kate was paralyzed. His eyes were strange, terrifying, lit with feral excitement. He tore at the bodice of her dress, pulled her face close to his, covering it with teeth marks and slobbering kisses. Nauseated, she tried to push him away. He whipsawed her across the face repeatedly, sending her sprawling against a sewing table. He was on her again, forcing his tongue between her lips like a rapier, fondling her breasts where he had torn away her dress, laughing hysterically at her mournful pleas.

Peterbroome began loosening his trousers, when Kate finally succeeded in pulling away. She screamed, pounding on him. He put his hands around her throat and began to tighten them, the look on his face wild, out of control.

Chapter Thirty-one

Nick, bored to the ears, left Charlie watching a game of billiards at Brooks and started for home. The delights of the club, which normally absorbed him, were like everything else these days, a shadow of their former amusement.

All day he felt uneasy and restless. Unable to concentrate on the work that had been left unattended since his mother arrived, complicated now by her decision to leave England, he decided to take a walk and found himself at the Grovenor house. He tried to gain entrance, and was turned away the same way his flowers had been received. Before leaving, he went around hoping to find Barkley. The big man was agitated, and asked him to leave at once. Kate was being watched, and Barkley was afraid he would be caught talking to Nick and lose the chance to help Kate.

Ten days had passed since the magical night in the garden, the very thought of which sent Nick's senses careening. Kate had said she loved him, of that there was no mistake. She returned his kisses as ardently as any man could wish. He knew she felt the same ecstasy as he. The memory of the few minutes of abandon, until he realized the hopelessness of it all and pushed her away, made sleeping and eating impossible.

Nick shrugged helplessly and left Brooks. Refusing a cab, he walked in the light mist to South Audley Street. He was taking the steps two at a time when a figure came out of the darkness. Nick backed down the steps, unsheathing the rapier hidden in his cane.

"It's me, sir, Barkley."

"You scared me half to death." Nick replaced the sword.

He opened the door and Kate's henchman followed him to the office. Barkley was white as a sheet and drenched to the skin.

"How long were you out there?" Nick asked, alarmed at the way the man was behaving.

"Hours." Barkley accepted a glass of brandy. "You said you wanted to help Lady Kate?"

"What happened?"

"I found out Peterbroome tried to rape my mistress, and damn near succeeded," he said, his voice breaking on the words. "Only the butler pounding on the door with a message saved my poor lady."

Nick loosened off a string of curses.

"I'll kill the son of a bitch, I swear it," he shouted, throwing his glass in the grate and preparing to leave the room.

"Hold up, sir," Barkley pleaded. "If any man kills Peterbroome, it will be me."

While they argued, the door swung open. Mrs. Monroe stood like a wraith in a white billowing nightdress, a letter dangling in her hand.

"I heard it all," she said in a calming voice. "Use your loafs, both of you. The man is protected on all sides by privilege and money. They will hound you down and kill you out of hand."

"I don't care," Nick said, attempting to push his mother aside.

"You, of all people, who saw how criminals are treated, should care. How will killing Peterbroome help Lady Katherine in the end?"

"It would be everything," the men declared at the same time.

"There will be a scandal, and her ladyship's father will be involved, the scandal out in the open. That will serve to blacken her name just as surely as if word got out that her father had been caught cheating."

"How did you know that Grovenor had been accused of cheating at cards, and Peterbroome was protecting him?"

Mrs. Monroe shrugged and sat down before the small fire.

"Charlie Slayton," Nick yelled. "I'll have his guts for garters."

The shock of the news sent Barkley back, and he fell heavily into a chair. Realizing that he was sitting in the presence of gentle folk, he sprang up in confusion.

"What you just learned is for your ears only," Nick warned the servant. "Understood?"

Barkley nodded.

Vivian Monroe went to the drinks table and refilled glasses for the men and one for herself. She remembered the letter, and handed it to Nick.

"This came for you earlier tonight."

Nick tore open the seal and read the note.

"The dog can talk."

Chapter Thirty-two

Kate lay huddled in a corner of her bed, her face still swollen and painful from Peterbroome's beating, her body bruised and sore. But more than anything was the shame and degradation she felt even hours after the assault.

When she had screamed seconds before the butler intervened, Peterbroome grinned lasciviously and clamped his hand over her mouth.

"Who are you going to tell what I have done to you?" He gloated. "I can always say you invited me here, and you know I will say exactly that, don't you? I don't care about my reputation. Talk of scandal is as good as the fact of it, my dear. But I'll kill you if you take up with any man."

All her fears about her marriage were no longer vague imaginings. Peterbroome would never be content to allow her a life of her own after she gave him an heir. Other women might do their duty as society saw it and kick over the traces, but not with someone as wildly possessive as Peterbroome. He might not love her, but that didn't mean he would allow another man to look at her with desire.

Kate pounded the bed at the memory of the utterly despicable afternoon. Despite being saved from the final indignity, she knew it would happen again, perhaps regularly, once she was Peterbroome's to command. She would never have defenses against anything Peterbroome wanted to do to her.

Kate trembled and hid her face in the pillows, futility bearing down on her like a rock.

*   *   *

The next morning, Nick and Charlie arrived at Tarn Maitland's house a half hour before the time Captain Black and White's letter instructed.

As soon as he read Tarn's letter, Nick fired off a note to Charlie to meet him at Manchester Square. He spent the rest of the night pacing and drinking until dawn. Ten times only Maitland's cryptic note kept him from storming out of the house bent on murdering Peterbroome. His mother's instructions, while sensible, were almost impossible to follow. Patience and injustice were two things he couldn't abide. Toward dawn he nodded off in a chair until an idea came to him. He went to his desk to write notes and draw plans on large pieces of parchment. Nick was grateful for the activity. It gave him a measure of peace, but not contentment. He knew with certainty that he had come up with an idea that could give Kate something of great and lasting value.

"You look a lot better than I expected," Slayton noted, when the two met outside Maitland's door the next morning.

Before Nick could reply, Maitland's butler noticed them pacing in front of the house. He came out and ushered them into the morning room. In the background they heard the squealing of children and Maitland's voice even louder than the rest. In a few minutes twin boys of four came into the room to use Nick and Charlie as shields.

It was a scene Nick never expected to see. The honored, dignified Captain Maitland, his ebony hair on end, dressed as a pirate. He picked his sons up and settled them under each arm.

"Ah, me hearties," Tarn said, laughing, "have a cup or two of tea, and I shall be with you presently."

Nick's impatience dissipated, giving way to wonderment.

"Will we ever be so fortunate?" Nick asked Charlie, listening to the laughs and protests from Tarn's captives down the hall.

"My dear Nick. First you make me a dull sober and reformed gambler, and now you suggest I try fatherhood. It's not on, old boy."

Nick had never thought much about fathering children, much less marriage, before a very special queenly-looking, red-haired, woman came into his life and turned it into a Greek tragedy.

"What are you thinking about, Nick?"

"How much some of my closest held ideas about life are dropping like tenpins."

Charlie was about to ask Nick to explain, when a short man in a black suit, who looked like a preacher, came into the room. He had the most mischievous eyes, and lit up the bright sun-filled room.

"Welcome, gentlemen. I am Bart Bolt, the captain's deputy." He smiled benevolently, adding to the impression of a kindly, well-dressed vicar. "I was ordered by him to investigate your feeling that there might be something havey-cavey about the Peterbroome betrothal."

He handed them each a document, called for tea to be served, and went to sit quietly with a book in the corner of the room overlooking a walled garden.

Nick and Charlie devoured the papers, registering shock and excitement along the way. When they finished, and almost on cue, Maitland appeared, immaculate in black-and-white riding clothes, a huge grin across his handsome face.

Nick, his voice thick with feeling, was the first to speak. "It says here that Grovenor did not cheat at cards!"

"He couldn't stack cordwood, much less a deck of cards in the state he was in. He was plied with liquor, and God knows what else, and allowed to win, as those affidavits testify," Maitland said, taking a chair and lighting a cheroot. "Just before he was comatose, they began blathering about cheating, and before the befuddled fool knew it, he had an insurrection on his hands,"

"They promised him scandal, disgrace, the usual, and were ready to hang him," Bolt said, taking up the narrative. "Peterbroome, conveniently close by, was called in to dampen matters. He persuaded, as one witness put it, to call a moratorium."

From the papers in front of him, Nick knew that the next day Peterbroome had confronted Grovenor. For a consideration of 10,000 pounds for each man, the other players promised to forget the incident and give their individual pledges to Peterbroome to keep quiet.

"But surely Grovenor must have known he didn't cheat and that the charges were trumped up. Why didn't he call them on it?" Nick asked, incredulous that such a scam could have succeeded.

"Apparently Peterbroome has a favorite maxim," Bolt interposed. "Talk of scandal is as bad as the act itself, if properly disseminated in the *ton*," Maitland said angrily. "Sadly, we hear, Grovenor isn't the only fool who has let Peterbroome and his merry band get away with such tactics in the past."

"But how did squashing the supposed scandal lead to Peterbroome's marriage to Kate?" Charlie asked.

"Peterbroome said all he wanted for saving Grovenor's reputation was marriage to Lady Katherine," Bolt explained.

"They hate each other, and have since childhood," Nick protested.

"Kate told me Peterbroome's grandfather insists that he marry her, and only her," Charlie added. "Isn't that true, either?"

Maitland and Bolt exchanged glances.

"What is it, Captain?" Nick was insistent.

"Peterbroome's grandfather is past caring whom he marries. He disowned him two months ago in favor of a cousin Peterbroome hates," Maitland said. "The need to marry well and quickly before the *ton* learned of this was pressing him from all sides."

Nick rose from his chair and prowled the room. Things began to fall into place. Nothing was what it was supposed to be in this sordid story.

"Kate was perfect for his scheme." Maitland went on. "Somehow Peterbroome learned that Kate inherits the Grovenor estate upon her father's death. The family will provides a woman can inherit."

Nick strode over to Maitland, his face contorted with rage.

"Very neat. He entangles Kate's father in a scandal he knows the old man hasn't the guts to fight, and then forces him to give Kate's hand in marriage. In return, he hushes thing up," Nick said, following Maitland's drift.

"The *ton* hates Pearson Grovenor and would make a meal for a week on rumors and innuendo," Charlie said, taking up the argument. "By the time the truth came out, my dear uncle would have been damned and the butt of all jokes. He hadn't the nerve to stand up to Peterbroome. People are frightened of him."

"That was what Peterbroome was counting on," Bart Bolt said quietly from his end of the room. "He is a very evil and resourceful man when he is cornered."

Nick swung around and looked closely from Bolt to Captain Black and White, catching a significant glance between the two men. His heart tilted in his chest.

"What would have stopped Peterbroome from killing Grovenor in a year or so and then, when the estate came into Kate's hands, killing her, too?"

"Exactly," Maitland replied coolly.

Charlie looked wildly around the room, unable to take in all that the others were saying. The lethal possibilities that had lain in wait for his beloved Kate had the marriage taken place made him shiver.

"The diabolical bastard. I'll have his heart," Nick said, falling heavily into a chair.

Chapter Thirty-three

It was three weeks after Kate's life had been saved.

Kate admitted it was an extravagant way to put her final extrication from Peterbroome's greedy and malevolent plot for her future, but it described her feelings to a nicety.

Her father was celebrating the freedom that Maitland's disclosures had given him by staying drunk for days. He spent the entire 40,000 pounds his erstwhile card-playing friends and Peterbroome's pawns returned to him on riotous parties, gifts for all and sundry ladies, and any mindless schemes that took his fancy.

He rarely saw Kate, and she was certain he avoided her. She was glad of it. They had nothing to give each other.

Peterbroome, after an earthy and painful encounter with Nick's fists, disappeared from sight. Word was that he was rusticating in the country. Most insiders, although not privy to all the facts, knew that after seeking the aid of St. Bart's Dr. William Lawrence, a surgeon famous for his healing skills, it was deemed advisable that he absent himself from the capital for a few months.

Kate's father's terse notice in the London papers announcing the betrothal was broken off by mutual consent was duly noted by the *ton*. Again without knowing the facts, everyone told everyone else they had known all along the engagement would not last.

Kate sat at a window. If I am at last truly rescued from Peterbroome, why am I still heart heavy and miserable? She knew, of course, but was afraid to face it. Instead she held her breath every time the doorbell rang, searched through the new and more extravagant flowers that were delivered daily now that she was disentangled, only to be terribly disappointed. There was affection aplenty in the cards that accompanied the floral offerings, but the one she wanted to receive never came.

It was as if Nick Monroe disappeared from her life.

Why didn't he come?

The thought of him, the memory of his strong, tapering fingers on her throat, caressing her breasts, his lips on hers, his body molded and pulsating against her, filled her days and nights with exquisite excitement and painful emptiness afterward. She needed and wanted fulfillment. She wanted Nick.

His continued silence only confirmed what Kate had known from the night in the Duchess of Gloucester's garden. He didn't want her; didn't love her; was disgusted by her.

Was she, indeed, repeating history? Once, as a child, Kate heard her father call her mother nothing more than a rutting cat, who needed every man who came down her alley. Kate was nine years old, innocent as a babe, and didn't know what her father meant. But now Kate knew only too well. Was she, at the end of the day, as wayward as Deidre Grovenor, a veritable kennel of cats?

And yet Kate could have sworn that on those few occasions when his nearness drove her to throw herself at his head, Nick seemed as lost in feeling as she was.

Oh, no, Kate, that's delusion . . . worse . . . self-delusion, she told herself. Look at it for what it is. He loves someone else, and Peterbroome or no Peterbroome, Nick's love for the phantom woman is real and constant.

Didn't Charlie say from the beginning Nick wanted to become the consummate gentleman for this woman? Well, he was the ultimate gentleman now. Indeed, the phenomenally popular toast of London and, rarity of rarities, an outsider accepted in some of the highest circles in London. Whatever happened, she could always take pride in the part she played in his success. It was cold comfort, and Kate shivered.

Better women than she wanted to die of unrequited love.

Why should she, the great Lady Katherine Grovenor, be immune from suffering now that she finally knew what it was to love with all her heart and body?

Tears, long repressed, threatened to choke her, but she fought them down. Kate rose from the chaise longue in her bedroom and went to the enormous cheval mirror. She studied herself with a fierce and critical eye. Self-pity didn't suit her at all.

Basta! Enough! It was time to resume living. Perhaps Herr Hendricks could find a role for her that required first-hand knowledge of a broken heart. Acting had made her happy, given her fulfillment. Why not now, when she needed it as never before?

Chapter Thirty-four

"When the hell are you going to call on Kate?"

"I refuse to discuss it," Nick said for the tenth time. It seemed the only subject he and Charlie could talk about since the day Maitland set in motion the end of Peterbroome's dominance over Kate and her father.

Maybe it's just as well, Charlie thought. From what he could tell, Kate didn't want to see Nick either. When he suggested that she write to Nick, she nearly brained him with a teapot. He wanted to bestir one or the other of them to make the first move, and would use any device to accomplish it, and more, Charlie wanted to revive the lovely life they had when they were united in hating Peterbroome and making Nick over. Now that Peterbroome was clear of the field, new problems arose.

Nothing seemed at all the same between Nick and himself, Charlie lamented. Worse still, he didn't know how they could resume the old footing. Once they were inseparable. A day counted as a dead loss if they didn't ride or dine together. Now it was rare for Nick to agree to see him, and then always at the Monroe home. Invitations to parties and events of the season's busy calendar were stacked on Nick's mantel and tucked into the mirror. Most, he suspected, weren't opened.

Kate was not unlike Nick in her refusal to be entertained. Going about the town without either one was dreary, but Charlie soldiered on. He had to have something to talk about when they agreed to see him.

"I think you owe Kate some explanation for your silence." Charlie was trying another tack.

"Kate's free to be happy, and that's all I ever wanted for her," Nick said in a low, tired voice. "You have known that from the beginning."

"What I have known and kept to myself is that each of you is mad about the other."

Nick came to life suddenly, rising from the chair behind his desk and sending it crashing against the window.

"You never told Kate how I feel, have you?" Nick demanded.

"I didn't, and I won't, but only because you insist," Charlie answered, shaken by his friend's sudden fury.

"How odd you are, Charlie," Nick said, wearily resuming his place at the desk, his fears allayed. "Once you begged me not to even consider wanting or dreaming of Kate, and now you want me to tell her I love her. Make up your mind, boyo. I am even less eligible as a husband to Kate than I have ever been."

Charlie wanted the two people he cherished over all others to be happy together, and at the moment they were miserable separately. He was at a loss to change matters.

"Kate will get over all this nonsense and find a good man," Nick said, the very thought making him ill.

"I hate it when people become resigned and philosophical," Charlie said, now perched on the end of Nick's desk.

"Marrying me would be going from the fire into the frying pan—" Nick said. In truth, he rather thought the idea spectacular, but that only happened when he was exhausted as he was now and his mind and conscience dulled.

"Nick, your father is dead. You're alive. You have earned your happiness," Charlie interrupted. "Maitland and Browning, the best of men, will never reveal your secret, nor I, of course, if that worries you."

Nick smiled gratefully. Until Kate came into his life, Nick didn't give a damn if anyone knew about his father. He had long been armed in his heart and soul by the certainty that his father was innocent, a victim of a terrible miscarriage of justice. It was Nick's greatest strength against a hostile world, a spur to his ambitions, and explained his easy sympathy for people less fortunate than he.

But things had changed radically in the last few weeks, and could not be denied.

The specter of his father's guilt made all his dreams of a life with Kate even more impossible. He could never ask Kate to share his life. Better to go away and start all over someplace else, knowing he had done the right and proper thing for her.

In truth, his future in England was hopeless. Neither his mother nor Charlie knew the latest threat, and, with luck, never would.

The week before, Nick received word that wily, old Delacourt family solicitor, Winters, was going to question some aspects of the sale of the estate. The family had been appalled that he sold the estate so cheaply. Nick told his man of business to settle the issue at once. He had no wish to punish Winters or the Delacourt family any longer.

No. Matters were not as simple as they once seemed.

Charlie roamed the room, waiting for Nick to come out from behind the funk that seemed to have overtaken him again. He spied a heavy trunk upended in the corner and went to investigate. It was a painful reminder that Nick was really leaving.

"Charlie, I almost forgot you were here."

"Do you mean to leave England without seeing Kate?"

Nick laughed in spite of himself. Charlie was nothing if not persistent. Nick stood, towering above the desk overflowing with charts and drawings, lists of figures, and, most prominent, the original plans of Delacourt House. Nick turned to the windows and looked out on the gathering dusk, rubbing his eyes.

"When I have something to tell Kate—and I will very soon—I will see her," Nick said with finality. "And I hope that will be in the next few days."

Charlie wanted to protest the news of the Monroes' departure once more, but knew it was useless.

"Lord Charles"—Mrs. Monroe came into the room— "please join us for dinner. My son is too solemn to be pleasant company."

Once dining at his various clubs or the hotels catering to

his circle had been a highlight of his life, after gambling and drinking. Now they were beginning to pall on him. Charlie was happy to have an alternative, and he readily agreed. The threesome removed to the drawing room for a preprandial sherry.

Dinner was a dreary affair. With all his skill at making himself charming to Mrs. Monroe, Charlie couldn't move a morose and silent Nick, no matter how he tried.

"Has Nick discussed his plans to keep you out of trouble after we leave?" Vivian Monroe asked over the fish. Charlie had been candid with her about his debt to Nick, and she knew and approved her son's generosity. After all, it was nothing more than she had taught him.

"Mam, that really is between Lord Charles and me," Nick protested.

Charlie coughed in his wine. "I haven't a clue, and to be honest, I have been concerned about it," Charlie offered. Talk of the money he still owed Nick for helping him pay his debts was very difficult at the best of times. He had little experience, for among his gentlemen friends talk of money was considered not quite the thing.

"Since it's been broached," Nick said, making the best of his mother's increasingly irksome interference, "I have plans, and mean to tell them to you in my own time. Briefly, I wish you to accompany me to New York next year and learn my business."

Charlie was speechless. This was a chance of a lifetime.

It was a mark of all that Nick had done for him that Charlie was honored and excited at the prospect of going into trade. How far he had come; how far he had matured. Before Nick changed his life, he would have been appalled at the idea of sullying his hands in commerce. Now he was eager to test his mettle, to be completely free of his family's disdain for him. He was becoming his own man, and looked eagerly up at Nick. He wanted to start to earn his keep as soon as possible. He was about to thank him, when the butler handed Nick a tray with a creased and filthy note on it. Nick read it, and a smile lit his brooding face.

"How much time will you need?" the note asked. Nick folded it, a Cheshire cat smile diffusing his face.

"This calls for champagne, the best in the house, Atkins," Nick ordered.

Charlie and Mrs. Monroe glanced at each other. Both were dying to know about the contents of the note that had caused the tidal change, but both knew better than to ask. Nick was beaming, and the dinner went on in fine style. Mrs. Monroe, a heart lightened by the new Nick she saw across the table from her, eventually left them to their port and cigars.

Mrs. Monroe had pushed and pulled Nick to sell Delacourt House and sever all his other ties to England, and wanted to know when, where, and how they were leaving. She knew he was growing tired of her endless questions, but that didn't concern her. It was her profound belief, and the reason she was so demanding, that Nick would once again be himself when time and distance widened between him and Katherine Grovenor. To see Nick showing his old self at dinner was wonderful, and she felt she could retire for the night happy. Once at home, she would begin looking for a suitable daughter-in-law, the very idea giving her all the more reason to show London the back of her heels.

Nick rose to call the butler and escorted his mother to the door.

"I say, Charlie, where are the Maitlands and the Brownings likely to be with their wives this night?" Nick asked casually, resuming his chair.

"Let me see." Charlie laughed, and extracted a number of invitations from the inside pocket of his brown velvet coat. The prospect of being on the town with Nick like the old days, was exhilarating. "The Londonderrys, Sally Jersey, and the Ord-Wades are all entertaining tonight."

"We should find them at one of these," Nick said, finishing the last of his port. "Now all we need is time for you to go home and dress."

Charlie approved Nick's return to enthusiasm, and said so.

"By the by, what the hell was in that note anyway?"

Charlie dared to ask. Expecting a sharp setdown, he was delighted when Nick passed it to him across the polished mahogany table.

Charlie read the unsigned, cryptic message, and was none the wiser. He looked to Nick for an explanation.

"Wish me luck. And if I don't fail, you will know in good time."

Nick saw Charlie off home and returned to his office to hastily scribble a reply to the man who sent him the note. He dressed in his finest evening clothes, bade his mother a warm good night, and left the house.

He waited for Charlie outside the Albany, sitting in his sprightly black cabriolet. The small, beautifully-sprung carriage was one of two Nick decided to take with him back to Australia. He had spent hours deciding what to do with his new possessions. He held long discussions with Tattersall's experts for what he hoped was the beginning of the Monroe stud, and gave orders for other cattle to be shipped later. A number of things made for Delacourt House would be transported to Sydney on the same ship he and his mother were taking.

Nick was planning a stately mansion, designed for him by London's finest architects, at the very moment. It would be more wonderful than Scottish Captain John Piper's Henrietta Villa, the only mansion of note in all of Australia, which overlooked the harbor in Sydney. Most of the larger pieces of furniture and oddments bought for Delacourt House at Kate's recommendation would remain. He hoped the new owner would love them as he did in the short time he had lived with their beauty.

Nick had about forgotten where he was. He did that a great deal lately, and it was disturbing, making him wonder if he would ever be himself again. He must leave off dreaming and melancholy introspection. And most of all forget the ever-present lilac scent and the voluptuous outlines of a woman who had made him rise to the heights of love and the depths of loss. He counted heavily on a change of scenery.

Charlie swung into the carriage with a jaunty air. He was back in spirits, and his usual impatient self.

"Spring the horses, old son. London at night awaits us."

Their luck was out at the first two parties. Neither the Maitlands nor the Brownings were seen or expected. With less pleasure than when they started, Nick and Charlie arrived at Lady Sally Jersey's house in the early hours of the morning. They made their addresses to their famous hostess, and paraded about the house.

To their surprise, Kate was present and dancing, her feet flying in silver slippers and her voluminous skirts swirling about. She glittered and outshone all the other women. Kate and her partner, a gigantic, handsome, redheaded Scotsman in full clan regalia, his eyes riveted on her glowing face, were advancing to the top of the line for the reel. All attention was centered in admiration of Kate and her Scot laird.

So much for Charlie's assertion that Kate had abandoned society and was pining for him, Nick noted angrily. What a laugh. The Scotsman with Kate was as bowled over by her, as Nick was himself. She had never looked so vivid or alluring. Was she playing a role? If so, who was she now?

He had come to the party to seek aid to bring Kate out of herself, and here she was having the time of her life without his or anyone's help. He looked around for Charlie. He wanted to leave, and before dawn, he promised himself, all outstanding plans to return to Australia would be set in gear. Whatever it was that made him put off his departure, the shilly-shallying he had been doing that drove his mother wild, was now at an end. Despite knowing how impossible it was, he had been secretly hoping against hope that something would happen to enable him to remain in England. What an idiot he was. Kate and her big Scotsman had proven it to him.

Going in search of Charlie, he ran into Kate and her escort on their way to the supper rooms.

"Mr. Monroe, how nice to see you again," Kate said, gaily offering her hand and introducing her Scotsman. He felt chilled and sick. How long was she going to haunt him? How was he going to live without her?

Kate's eyes lost some of their magical glint, and her smile was less dazzling than during the dance, but Nick didn't see the changes. He bowed and kissed Kate's out-stretched hand. He felt a fire between them, and put it down to his overheated imagination. Well, that would go away. It must. This hour a few days from now he would be sailing out of England and to a life without Kate.

"I hope you are well and much relieved by events," Nick said, his voice pitched low, trying to be formal as well as circumspect.

"I feel quite joyous, Mr. Monroe," Kate said, her heart beating harder than ever at the sight of him. There was no freedom without Nick. Who was she trying to deceive, Nick or herself? He was more wonderful looking than ever, so vital that even the merry, stalwart fellow beside her paled in comparison. For all her resolution to forget Nick Monroe, to live however she wanted to in the future, the truth was she had nothing without him.

"I am so happy for you, my lady," Nick said formally, bowing again to her and her dance partner. He resumed his search for Charlie, and found him talking animatedly to Barbara Maitland and Colby Browning in a corner of a small room, their heads close together. He felt de trop, and was turning away when Lady Barbara beckoned to him.

"I was coming for you, Nick," Charlie said, his eyes blazing. "The ladies were just telling me that Pearson Grovenor is planning to marry a much younger woman, Miss Gladys Springer of York, and set up a nursery as soon as he can."

"If that happens, Kate will no longer be the sole heir to the Grovenor estate, and her father can be generous or penurious—and we all feel it will be the latter," Lady Barbara lamented. "That man is a fiend. Again he is putting Kate into an untenable situation. Something must be done for Kate, and soon."

"Lady Katherine doesn't seem very perturbed about the

prospect. Why should you?" Nick was remembering Kate's abandon on the dance floor.

"Don't you realize she is a better actress than anyone treading the boards at Drury Lane?" Lady Barbara chided him.

I know better than all of you what a great actress she is, Nick wanted to shout, but it was still his and Kate's secret.

"You are as blind as most men are where their women are concerned," Barbara Maitland said, out of patience with them. "I don't know what it is that drives Kate, but she is far from indifferent to all that has happened to her. Lady Colby and I have known she was unhappy for a long time. Between Peterbroome and her father, it is a wonder she is still sane. And now this new absurdity. She will soon be forced to marry for security. It is a terrible thought."

"If Grovenor's young wife produces an heir, Kate will be virtually penniless. We all know her father is a heavy toper and gambles like a demon. My cousin Kate has a lot to worry about," Charlie threw in.

Nick was at once on the alert. Kate, off the dance floor, seemed older, slimmer, even a little worn about the mouth. She appeared, now that he thought about it, on the verge of tears. Where the hell were your eyes? Nick demanded.

"Lady Colby and I are at our wits' end. We have tried to befriend her, and seemed to be succeeding in having her join us in our charities, but the last few weeks she has been incommunicado."

All the reasons he had originally wanted to consult, the Maitland and Browning ladies reanimated in Nick. He was taking a big risk, and he knew it, but he saw no other way out of this latest dilemma. More than ever Kate needed a friend, and this would be his final and, possibly, his best service to her.

"Have you and Lady Colby any plans for a public charity any time soon?" Nick asked casually, keeping his fingers crossed.

"We always have plans, my dear Mr. Monroe, but these public occasions are so volatile, one is quite exhausted coming up with new ideas to separate the *ton* from their money."

Still Nick hesitated. Had he the right to disclose Kate's secret life and talents? He decided he did.

"Do you, Lady Barbara, Lady Colby, and Charlie really have Lady Kate's interests at heart, or is it all drawing-room talk?" Nick asked bluntly, throwing them into confusion.

"That is an impertinent question, Nick," Charlie was quick to say.

"No. It isn't. I must swear you to secrecy no matter what happens, because someone's reputation is at stake, and I am desperate enough to put her at risk."

The three looked at him puzzled, but agreed at once.

"If what you suggest is designed to help Kate, you have our full cooperation." Lady Colby spoke up in her usual forceful way.

"Leave it with me," Nick said happily. "I have several things in mind. You may have to humor me, however. Be prepared to act upon my orders immediately."

The three were intrigued and wanted more details, but Nick was adamant.

"If you do exactly as I ask, I will make your favorite charity a gift of 1,000 pounds at once. In gold, in fact." At last he could respond wholeheartedly to the question asked in the note given to him at dinner that night.

Chapter Thirty-five

Nick went about the last-minute rush to leave England with the same fanatical attention to detail that marked all his endeavors.

At the same time a stream of men and women strolled in and out of South Audley Street who seemed far removed from anything having to do with the Monroes' imminent departure.

"Really, Nick, this mysteriousness of yours is very trying." Vivian Monroe challenged him on the third day. "The house is in a stew. I would like an explanation."

Nick smiled enigmatically and tried to fob her off with evasions until Vivian Monroe went too far.

"I demand to know what all these people are about," she said at breakfast one morning. "Why do I think this has something to do with Kate Grovenor?"

Nick was tired and angry. The closer their leaving, the more depressed he became.

"I have tried not to think about the lengths you have gone to separate me from Kate," Nick said coldly. "You inveigled Charlie in your cabal, and steadily reminded me of my unsuitability as a husband. Well, you have succeeded. Enjoy your victory, and leave me in peace."

The atmosphere went from chill to ice, and was so unlike them that neither mother nor son knew how to reach each other.

Across the city, Kate circled the huge dining table for the fifth time. Spread on the table were drawings and miniature stage settings for Herr Hendricks's latest production.

"I can't afford to stage this," Kate groaned. "When I said I wanted to work again, I meant our usual modest scene or two."

"I am happy to tell you that for once I do not need your money, dear Lady Katherine."

"But where did the money come from?" Kate asked, looking over at the plans again. The very simplicity of the scenery was stunning, the creation of an imaginative hand.

The little hunchback moved to take Kate's hand. "A man who knew my work in Germany wishes me to return, but wants to see something new of mine. One act is all he wants to see."

"You did not tell me anyone was to attend the play." Kate reared back in alarm. "It has always been our agreement that no one watches me."

The man began to sweat, trying to remember exactly what Nick had told him to say. "My dear, be reasonable. The man wants to see what he is putting his money into. Can you blame him?"

Kate walked around the table once more and smiled at the man. To appear on a stage with real scenery, wasn't this what she had always wanted? Besides, what had she to lose? Her reputation? Her place in society? These things held no threat or meaning any longer.

Wasn't she, in fact, a joke, a cruel joke? Years on the town, and what did she have to show for it? Men wanted to marry her, and she had spurned them out of hand, not knowing or understanding what she did to them; one failed betrothal to a rogue of lineage; a father who threw her to the winds once her usefulness was over and now was going to marry a woman to give him a male heir; and, finally, not enough money of her own to buy herself a hat. She would soon be holding out for a rich husband. What a well-deserved comedown for the high-and-mighty Lady Katherine Grovenor.

And what of the man she loved beyond life itself leaving England without a backward glance?

Kate came around the table and threw her arms around her teacher and her friend.

"When shall you want me to be ready, Herr Hendricks?"

The old man teetered against Kate. He had never dreamed she would accept so easily.

"Today is Monday. Can you be ready by Friday?"

Kate took the playscript he offered her and held it to her breast.

"I will be ready. I promise."

Chapter Thirty-six

Nick arrived an hour before everyone was expected. A little of the theater's long-gone grandeur had been cosmetically and quickly restored in front and behind the stage. He was pleased that his orders had been carried out to the letter.

Still he was edgy. He told Barkley to arrive with Kate fifteen minutes before the performance, although he still couldn't believe Kate had succumbed to his elaborate charade quite as easily as Herr Hendricks said.

"You don't know actresses," the director crowed. "The chance to perform against such exquisite scenery in a fabulous gown such as you designed was irresistible."

And now the night he'd planned in minute detail arrived. Kate's future was in the balance, his parting gift to her about to have a life of its own.

Rain began falling just as the Grovenor carriage, with its now familiar crest gleaming on the door, entered the alley at the side of the theater, giving Nick a sharp pang of memory. He slipped quickly into the shadows, just as he had on that first night.

A few minutes later a small, closed carriage arrived at the entrance of the theater, dislodging Lady Barbara and Lady Colby, with Charlie in attendance. Nick was at the door to caution them to be quiet, and ushered them into a back row where they couldn't be seen from the stage.

With cape and dark hat as disguise, Nick walked midway down the aisle and fell into a seat, befitting the fictitious German Kate was expecting.

The small orchestra began playing a simple lament,

which Kate would reprise on a pianoforte waiting for her on stage.

The music, sad and aching, mirrored everything Kate was feeling. It seemed ages since she was truly content and on a stage, playing a part. The elaborate, jewel-encrusted costume made for the part of an Elizabethan lady of rank, waiting to say good-bye to her lover, and the lush scenery managed to encase Kate in a fantasy, shutting out the real world.

In the theater, Barbara, Colby, and Charlie shared the sense of mystery and high expectation that Nick promised. They awaited the performance with barely concealed excitement.

At once a woman of imperial manner and dress came onto the stage and made it her own. For the next half hour the audience of four was transfixed, speechless in fact.

When Nick slipped out, no one noticed, and that suited the next phase of his own drama.

Kate stumbled, exiting the stage, tears blurring her eyes.

"You were superb as usual," Nick said, offering her his handkerchief.

"What are you doing here?" Kate fell back in astonishment, looking around wildly, her first instinct to run and hide. He was the last person she expected to see.

"I thought I'd say good-bye," Nick replied, trying to burn his last look at Kate into his mind.

"What did you mean by 'as usual'?" Kate cried. "Have you seen me before?"

"Twice actually. But that isn't what I came to talk about," he said, handing her a folio. "I leave on the tide. In here are the deeds to Delacourt House, which I hope you will accept as your home and perhaps as a place where people might gather and enjoy all the arts that interest you. You know better than anyone how important it is to have a refuge, and Delacourt House is made for you."

Kate looked at Nick, not sure she understood, or even wanted to. Before she could find her voice, he held out his hand.

"You are truly free of your father or anyone who would

keep you from being yourself." Nick kissed her hand, turned it, and laid his cheek briefly against the palm.

He heard Charlie and the others in the background calling to her, and moved quickly, calling over his shoulder.

"Don't ever be afraid again, Kate. That's my real gift to you."

Finally aware the cold rain was running down his neck, Nick gathered the collar of his cloak close. He'd been walking for hours. He'd done the right thing. He'd given Kate the money and the means to be an actress or anything she wanted. If he thought that in the process he'd find solace for his own impossible dreams, he was wrong, and he knew it.

Tomorrow it would all be academic anyway. Once he and his mother arrived in Australia, he would settle her and see that the work on his house began. After that, he'd be off to New York to see to his financial interests and check on Charlie. Then he'd find still another place to waste time and appease his loneliness. The very thought brought Nick up short and made him take his bearings. He was within a few blocks of home, and proceeded quickly.

The blow came so fast, Nick fell backward like a log.

"Consider this my revenge for setting Maitland's men on me, Monroe."

Nick might be stunned, but he knew a professional hit when he felt one and wasn't surprised.

"And don't think he's finished with you." Nick heard the derisive laughter of several men. "He has a score to settle with you."

Peterbroome wasn't alone. Far from it.

Nick rose to one knee. He might not be a match for Peterbroome and his friends, but he was determined to give a good Australian account of himself.

A hand took his elbow and yanked him to his feet.

"Thanks," Nick said mechanically. "Now is it to be a round robin, or is it to be a fair fight? One at a time."

They laughed at him.

Nick saw the next jab coming and ducked, sending a

straight fist to the soft belly of the man who threw the punch, pivoting and taking on the next man, Peterbroome himself. They fell heavily to the ground, rolling in the dirt, the air redolent with oaths and curses with the bystanders making bets among themselves. Equally matched in height and skill, the damage was equal as well. Nick was able to rise on one knee and catch Peterbroome with a punishing right hand.

He flailed out at Nick and, missing him, called out, "My sword."

Nick saw the flash of a blade. Too late. He felt a sharp, cold thrust to his side, the life going out of his legs at the same time.

"You really are a bastard, John. This was only to be a bit of sport, not murder."

"How wrong you were, mate," Nick started to say. The words didn't quite make it to his lips.

Chapter Thirty-seven

Kate walked the carpet of the drawing room at South Audley Street, losing count after one hundred circuits.

It seemed an eternity between the time one of Maitland's men reported finding Nick and the time Maitland himself and Charlie arrived with a makeshift litter.

Nick was more dead than alive.

Dawn came and went, and still Kate walked. She was afraid to stop, afraid if she stopped Dr. Lawrence would come down and tell her Nick was dead. He had not come, nor had anyone else.

Nick's last coherent words to his rescuers were that Peterbroome stabbed him. Charlie, Maitland, Browning, and others were combing London in search of him. Mrs. Monroe was hysterical, and had to be sedated.

These few details of the night penetrated Kate's brain as she paced, her step more frantic with each passing hour.

The door opened.

"I've done all I can," Dr. Lawrence said, sinking into a chair. "I despair for him, my lady. Any other man would have been dead hours ago."

Kate stopped her pacing and patted the doctor's shoulder.

"He'll live," Kate said with perfect conviction, and left the room. She took the steps in a rush, and beckoned the nurse tending Nick to join her outside the door.

"I am going to lie down, and when I awake, I want you to show me how to take care of Mr. Monroe."

Everyone marveled at Kate's stamina and determination over the next weeks. Working night and day to care for

Nick, her strength seemed to grow. In the same way Kate's beauty was more luminous than ever. She never left his side, having a camp bed placed next to his bed.

Kate was plainly aware that Nick's mother and Nurse Wells thought the strain was beginning to take its toll. They told the doctor of Kate's strange actions. Looking in on Kate and Nick from time to time, they caught her sitting by the bedside holding Nick's hand, a steady spate of songs, poetry, doggerel, soft words washing over the room. They were worried and afraid to challenge Kate, and felt compelled to mention it to Dr. Lawrence.

He slipped into the room and heard for himself.

"It's all right, darling, no one will ever hurt you again. I promise," Kate was saying in song and caressing phrases.

She heard the door and looked up. She smiled sheepishly.

"Does it help you or the patient?" he asked kindly.

"I'm pulling him back from whatever place has him imprisoned."

The sense of peace and confidence she had in Nick's recovery began to infect everyone around them.

One night Kate was sitting beside Nick's bed, dozing over a book. She felt rather than saw him stir, and was instantly on guard.

"Kate, don't ever go away." Until then, he had not spoken a discernible word.

"Never, darling," she whispered, tears she'd held at bay soon spilling down her face. She bent over to place a gentle kiss on his forehead. Kate had learned early on all the things that seemed to quiet Nick when he was agitated. She stepped back as if burned. His forehead was hell hot, beads of perspiration clouding his eyes, open and staring blindly at her.

"What is it, my love?" Kate asked, willing him to hear her. "Are you in pain?"

Nick groaned and began to thrash on the bed, eluding all her efforts to hold him. Kate couldn't believe it. Twice in the month since the attack, he had fought back fevers and infections, and only that day she and the doctor were certain they had turned the corner. He had seemed free of danger, and now he was bad again, worse than ever.

"I'm cold," Nick cried, and she scoured the room to find blankets. When they didn't stop his convulsive shaking, Kate got into bed and held him like the baby she'd never had. She rocked and crooned, her arms holding him close, her tears falling on his cheek. Nick burrowed his head against her, racked by chills, burning with fever.

Kate took his hands, cupping them over her breasts, praying that the warmth swelling her loins and causing her head to swim would somehow be enough for the two of them. For all her distress, Kate wanted the moment never to end. She had never been so content. She was home. They lay together in the dimly lit and silent room, until, magically, she became aware that Nick's breathing was even, the shivering had passed, and he lay at peace in her arms.

Kate didn't hear the door open, everything about her concentrated on willing life into Nick.

"Is he dead?"

It was Vivian Monroe. She stood inside the room, afraid to go forward.

To be caught in bed with Nick by his mother, of all people, was terrible. The two had fought a raging battle over caring for Nick, and only Kate's iron will won the day.

"I woke an hour ago, and thought it was the end," the old lady moaned.

"I think he will recover." Kate slipped out of the bed as quietly as she could, afraid to disturb Nick.

The news brought Mrs. Monroe to the bed, the return of her antagonism in sharp contrast to the pitiful figure she made coming into the sickroom.

"Was getting into bed with my son quite necessary?" she asked tight-lipped. "I cannot imagine what Dr. Lawrence will have to say to that."

"Frankly, Mrs. Monroe, I thought it was the best medicine for your son at the time. And I don't give a damn what you or Dr. Lawrence or anyone has to say about me and Nick."

Kate turned to adjust Nick's covers, and to hide her tears.

"I have known from the beginning that you disapproved of my love for Nick," Kate said, turning around to face Mrs. Monroe. "If Nick wants me half as much as I want him, nothing on this green earth will stop us."

Nick's mother moved closer to the bed and saw for herself that Kate's prognosis was true. Nick looked frail and very white, but the essence of life was finally returning to his face. Vivian Monroe had her son back, and she'd fight for him as never before. She smiled cruelly at Kate, and moved away from the bed toward the door.

"You are very sure of yourself, my lady," she said, cold and sneering, "but how will you feel about marrying the son of a true convict, not the innocent story Nick told Charlie and all your famous friends? The truth will get out, and then watch your friends desert you. You will become as estranged from your world as I did from mine. It isn't a pretty picture."

"I am in love with a good man. If he'll have me, I will never run away from him, nor he from me. With respect, I can be just as determined as you are. Only Nick matters, and it would be well that you learn that."

They heard the rustle of linen behind them and saw Nick attempt to sit up. They rushed to the bed.

"Leave us, please, Mam," he said, and, gray-faced, fell back against the pillows.

Mrs. Monroe was about to argue, then turned and left abruptly.

"I'll have you, Kate," Nick murmured, a shadow of a smile on his bloodless lips. "Oh, God, I'll have you."

Chapter Thirty-eight

Nick Monroe looked out over the peaceful, perfectly undulating green lawn, the glory of two hundred years of loving care and vigorous rolling by succeeding generations of Delacourt gardeners.

The mist was rising with the sun. Nick turned and looked across to the bed.

"Put on a robe. I can't go through another sickbed vigil." Kate laughed, watching him. Her mass of long, indescribably lustrous hair barely covered her naked breasts, the nipples still engorged after a night of love.

Nick went weak at the sight of her. With mounds of white, silken pillows piled high behind and the bed coverings mounded before her, Kate was like a siren on a fleecy cloud beckoning to him. Two long strides, and he was on the bed beside her. Kate came into his arms and opened herself to his overpowering need.

They kissed and fondled, insatiable to the taste and core of the other. In the fourth day of their honeymoon, they knew all the ways to bring each other to the heights.

The world beyond the windows, society and its shibboleths could wait their pleasure in each other forever.